T0162634

GRANNY
FOR HIRE

Anne Welters

Order this book online at www.trafford.com
or email orders@trafford.com

Most Trafford titles are also available at major online book retailers.

Printed in the United States of America.

ISBN: 978-1-4669-6227-9 (sc)
ISBN: 978-1-4669-6229-3 (hc)
ISBN: 978-1-4669-6228-6 (e)

Library of Congress Control Number: 2012918819

Trafford rev. 10/11/2012

   www.trafford.com

North America & international
toll-free: 1 888 232 4444 (USA & Canada)
phone: 250 383 6864 ◆ fax: 812 355 4082

I dedicate this book to all those who feel lonely and forgotten ....
look inside yourself to free your spirit

Chapter One

I T WAS SUNDAY AGAIN. Ideally, a day of rest, and families, just chilling out but for Gail it loomed like a black cloud. First of all there was no reason to get up early.

Actually there was no reason to get up at all, but then again, maybe, just maybe, one of the children would call, or even visit. Just maybe, you never know, so she dressed hurriedly, just in case. She delayed her breakfast of cereal and tea just in case she was invited out for breakfast. But by midmorning, she reluctantly prepared her usual breakfast, and ate it sitting on the bar stool at the kitchen counter. She kept her telephone nearby where she could easily reach it if it rang.

The morning passed while Gail dusted and vacuumed, much like other days, and the phone never rang, and no one knocked on the front door although Gail kept hoping that it would happen. Lunch was never really planned for because she often thought that se would be invited out, so today it was a simple meal of toast, topped with cheese and a banana for keeping healthy, a squirt of syrup on top was to quell the sweet craving which Gail knew would rear its head around three or four.

After reading for a while with her reading glasses on her nose and holding a magnifying glass a few centimetres from the page in order to read the writing, she closed the book. She was bored and lonely, and she felt unwanted, unappreciated, and unloved. Oh! Gail knew that the children were probably busy, and with working so hard, they needed some time with their families, and this she understood and accepted, although a phone call would surely not take up so much time, and would mean a lot to her.

The chair was pulled up close to the window where the light was better for reading and rays of sunlight caused a warm feeling on her body.

The book lay closed on her lap and her eyes stared at the wall facing her, without really looking at it, as thoughts flitted through her mind. Surely there must be something that she could do to change her lifestyle? Wishes, or was it dreams floated in and out, and in and out, and then a thought flirted with her mind. Not once but repeatedly. The same thread kept moving around, or was it pulling? She was not sure which but somehow the thought got snared on a tiny barb in her brain and kept flashing until she took notice of it.

Gail lived on her own since the demise of her husband of forty-one years.

To be honest, although she enjoyed being her own boss, and doing what she wanted, and how she wanted, she missed him. The children, now grown with families of their own spent less and less time with her and she knew it was not because they did not love her, no she knew they did, but it was because they were so caught up in their own lives, that they forgot to contact her, and that was OK! Except a call now and again would be nice, or even an invitation to share a meal, or a cup of tea and cake, but she knew they were busy and that was OK! Was it not?

Of course, if Gail had any money in the bank, or the safe, or in any place like investments, it would have been easier. Maybe a package tour to some or other exotic land would be nice. After all, Gail always wanted to travel didn't she?

So here, on this quiet Sunday afternoon with the book on her lap and the suns' rays warning her body sitting by the window, an idea so bizarre, as to be most unfeasible, stuck in her mind and was sending flashes like small lightning bolts through her that made Gail smile. Well, why ever not? What could she loose?

It surely will be of benefit not only to her, but for those who would make use of her services. Of course, nothing may come of it, but it was worth a try, after all, what did she have to lose, and who did she have to answer to?

Gail took a clean sheet of paper and drafted and advertisement.

She took some time to weigh up all her options and narrowed her skills down to the basics. She had to include her age which was a good age if you think that sixty-seven is a good age, but of course the job was for someone of a good age, and that she was. She was also experienced for the job of a granny, after all you had to be a granny, to become a granny and yes, you should have experience for the job and Gail definitely qualified. The job would require that you live in, but that Gail was prepared to do, and Gail was even prepared to travel to the place of employment, providing that such expenses were paid by the employer.

This goes without question of course, and naturally, Gail would expect to be paid a salary. After all, it would be like a proper job, but only more personal and of course Gail would expect it to be personal, for the relationship to work.

After a few drafts she settled on a simple advert that read

"Granny for Hire—I am experienced, with references and willing to travel".

She added her telephone number and after some thought added the international code and then another thought prompted her to look at other locations that would be suitable. If making a change was exactly that, then surely it would be exciting to target another country. She mulled over this decision, thinking of her as yet unused passport, locked in the safe. Full of dreams, she had applied for this when there was a glimmer of hope, or was it a dream, that she would visit Greece. Three years have since passed and the passport still had not been used. So she added another line to the draft which said "fluent in English and Afrikaans." She also added her e-mail address. Although she hated e-mails, after all you never knew what popped up, on the computer screen, so she reluctantly used it, seeing as everyone expected one to have such a facility.

Greece was where she had wanted to go to, but the language could be a problem, so Europe would probably be the best. She pinpointed two possibilities, Austria and France. If she had no response from these places she would broaden the field.

But first she had to find out how to go about placing and ad in the newspapers of those countries. This exercise she found out was actually quite simple. One telephoned the local newspapers and after reading the add and her credit card details, they assured her the ad would appear in the newspapers of those two countries, within a few days.

The next few days flew by as Gail checked her e-mails each evening after dinner. She had not said anything to the children. Not because no contact from any of them was forthcoming, but she did not know if her ad would have any success. After all, you never know if you wasted your money, what little you have, or your idea of course, or not, and that is why Gail never phoned them, especially when she knew they were so busy.

On the fourth day, Gail had made little ticks on the calendar, an e-mail message appeared and she held her breath as she clicked on the line to open the message.

"Dear Madam" the message started. "My name is Johan Gerber. I live with my three children, a girl aged eleven and two sons aged nine and six. My wife passed away seven months ago and the children are missing her a lot."

Her heart started to pound and she instinctively put her right hand to her breast, as she carried on reading.

"I saw your advertisement in our local newspaper and as we are South Africans working abroad I thought that a granny could help them. If you feel that this is so, please reply, as soon as possible. Kind regards Johan Gerber—Austria."

Her first instinct was to click on the reply button, but she hesitated, and got up and walked to the lounge where she sat on her chair near the window where a curtain now blocked out the night. Could this really be happening? What if this plan got off the ground, what, what?

There are so many what ifs, and she closed her eyes for a short while.

After seconds passed or was it minutes, Gail did not know for sure how long she sat there, she got up and went back to the computer. The next step had formulated in her mind and her fingers found the keys easily.

"Dear Mr Gerber" and here she paused, should she say Mr Gerber or should she say Johan? This hesitation did not last long and she left it as Mr Gerber, after all one did not want to be familiar with a stranger and that is after all what he was.

"I am a widow, aged 67. My children are all grown up with grown up families of their own and I decided that I could be of use to someone who needed me.

My age is of little importance as I am healthy and love to have children around me. Please let me have more details regarding your requirements.

Kind Regards, Gail Harper."

Two days went by of e-mails going back and forth and two other enquiries also came through during that time which was exciting for her as she was initially dubious about the whole idea. Goes to show, she thought, there is a market out there, for people whose 'sell by' date, had seriously expired.

Well, she was going to make this work for all parties concerned, her employer, his children and herself. The whole thing just felt so right that she felt a bit afraid that it was just a dream.

On the fourth day after the first communication, she still had not had a call from any of her children.

Gail realised that she would have to phone them to tell them about her plans. Thinking about it and everything that had to be done made her hands feel clammy and she was sure her heartbeat was faster. Tonight she would phone them but first she had to see her grandson Bernard to see if he would move into her home. She thought it could work well as he had recently got out of a sticky relationship and anyway he loved to be near the sea and his life passion was being on a surfboard.

First she thought she would just lock up the house and go. There was no guarantee that the job would pan out although on the other hand it would be foolish to leave the house unused if she was going to be away for any length of time.

Gail went to the place where he worked and after hearing what she had to say he was keen and the matter was settled.

"Hello" came he deep voice of Jake her eldest son. She loved, hearing his voice, it reminded her of her late husband who also had that timber in his voice.

"Hello Jake, how are you all."

"Oh, hi mom, haven't heard from you in a while, is everything OK?"

"I was wondering if you could perhaps come and visit soon" before he could make any excuse, Gail carried on "it is rather important and the matter is urgent."

After a slight hesitation he said "you are all right are you, do you need a doctor?"

"No, no" she said "but I have to see you all."

The next call to Gavin had a similar reaction, but visits from both sons could be expected within an hour. She would call Sarah after their visit as Sarah lived far away and it would not really be any different as visits to her only took place once or twice a year.

When the two brothers arrived more or less at the same time, Gail had all the documents ready. Once she started making arrangements there were actually quite a few official forms that had to be signed, like a will that had to be updated, and power of attorney forms in case something went wrong while she was away and visas and tickets that had to copied.

To lessen the impact which Gail knew would soon explode, she first served drinks all round and made small talk about their families and their work. When she casually said she would be away for a while they thought she was going to Sarah on holiday.

Slowly and methodically she laid her plans on the table. After a stunned silence Gavin was the first to speak.

"Why are you doing this Mom?"

A wistful smile softened Gail's face as she said "It feels good and I am looking forward to it." She knew she could never tell them how they neglected her.

More questions were asked and answered, and then the time came for the documents to be signed which caused more questions to be asked and more answers.

The next few days went by in a mad rush to pack all the personal things like clothes and photos that would be stored, and sorting through clothes that should be taken with or not. Gail thought about the conversation she had with Sarah and she felt a little sad as the relationship between them had been strained for a while. Somehow Gail knew that Sarah felt that she, Gail, thought she was not a good mother to her two rebellious sons.

This Gail felt, was because they were too indulged and given too much importance besides all the attention that was lavished on them. The total result was that the children gave their parents no respect or gratitude.

Gail also knew she could never point this out to Sarah who would again take it up the wrong way, so Gail said nothing, except to ask about their health, and wellbeing. Her own plans, when explained, were classed as unimportant to Sarah, as her attention was distracted by a demand of some kind from her eldest son. When Gail put the telephone down, she realised that Sarah actually had no idea why the phone call was made in the first place.

Well there was nothing Gail could do about that.

Chapter Two

AFTER THE COURIER HAD dropped Gail at the airport and she settled her luggage with a porter, who helped her to the airline, she was travelling with, she sat on a chair—a nice soft one—and watched the big planes on the tarmac. The whole thing felt like a dream to Gail and she actually felt very emotional.

There was no objection from Jake or Gavin when she told them that a courier would take her to the airport. This saddened her. Amazing how little anyone cared these days. She knew they were busy, but still it would have been nice to have one of her family members with her on this momentous occasion. Well, she would hopefully be going to a place where she would be needed, and this cheered her somewhat, but still, it would have been nice.

She was nervous, after all, she had never been out of her country before.

She applied for her passport nearly three years previously and never had the opportunity to use it.

So here she was, her travel tablet helped to keep her heart steady, although she knew that she would have to take another one later when she was settled in the plane, which was OK, she was fine with that, she hoped.

The size of the plane inside with its many people was awesome and once settled in her seat she unobtrusively scanned the faces nearest to her and tried to link a story to the face. So many travellers, where are they going, who will they meet?

Although daunted by the long hours she would be in the plane, Gail settled herself into a comfortable position. The take-off, after two tablets, was not quite as nerve racking as she imagined it would be.

She took a deep breath and relaxed. She had done all she could, said prayer after prayer for a safe journey and pleasant stay, and knowing the situation was now out her hands, she smiled. This was it! She was on her way. This was her adventure and she would live it, however it turned out to be.

Chapter Three

A FEELING OF PANIC FLASHED through her heart and it seemed to grow stronger by the second. For a fleeting moment she closed her eyes and sent a silent prayer for courage once again, and then she opened her eyes and smiled at the man holding up a board with her name on it. He took her trolley with her bags on it, and she followed him to a car where he opened the back door for her to get in.

The car was comfortable and the temperature was just right. Gail slowly, relaxed and once they left the airport she sat forward to look at the buildings they passed.

No conversation took place between her and the driver and she wondered if he could speak English so she asked.

"Excuse me, do you speak English?"

"Yes, Mrs Harper, I do."

"I am happy to hear that, could you please point out the places that we pass. You see, I have never been here before."

"With pleasure" he said and gave short descriptions of the buildings, as they drove by.

Gail enjoyed the drive and the information given by the driver kept her from thinking about her forthcoming meeting with her new family.

The driveway was not very long and the house at the end was large, but not, unpleasantly so. It had a flow to it like corn growing on he fields.

It was painted in soft earth ochre and had white trimming around the windows with a roof of brick coloured tiles.

When the driver opened her door, Gail smiled at him and she was sure she detected a faint smile from him. She got out and with a firm stride, which belied, the feeling of panic, within her walked to the door which opened before she could knock. In the doorway were three children looking all excited. They came to meet her and hugged her around her waist and knees. Completely taken by surprise she instinctively put her arms around the little group and then she was pulled inside.

The person that greeted Gail in the entrance was in her early thirties and had a friendly smile. In broken English she greeted Gail.

"Welcome to Austria, we are very happy to have you with us."

"Thank you, I am also so happy to be here."

"Please to join us for tea, my name is Ursula, I am housekeeper."

"My name is Gail" and looking at the children's faces, she said to them "and you can call me 'Site' and before you ask me why, I will tell you when we have our bedtime story tonight."

Giggling the children left the room.

The next half hour was pleasant as Ursula and Gail exchanged information about each other and then Ursula took Gail to her suite where her luggage was waiting for her. Ursula asked if she could help to unpack but Gail declined the offer as a sudden fatigue had come over her and she knew that the travelling had caught up with her.

As soon as Ursula left the room Gail pulled the bedcover down and only removed her shoes and jacket. As she lay down she instantly fell asleep.

When Gail opened her eyes she was confused as to where she was and noticed that a warm rug had been thrown over her. Slowly she rose and swung her legs over the edge of the bed and then she saw that her suitcases were stacked neatly above the cupboard and knew that her clothes would be unpacked, and the gesture made her feel welcome.

The suite was comfortable and big enough not to feel confined. Two large windows looked out over the front entrance and she saw a car parked in the paved parking bay flanking the entrance. It was, she noticed an expensive German car and it looked very new to her.

There were two doors leading off her bedroom and on opening one, she saw a pleasant bathroom with bath and shower. Her toiletries were neatly arranged on the cupboard next to the hand basin. The second door led into a private lounge area with a sofa and a comfortable armchair, as well as, a television placed on a low cupboard with pictures of the children in silver frames. A small writing desk with chair was placed under the window and a bookshelf was next to it.

Gail was pleased with her surroundings and with a flutter in her chest she felt that she had made the right decision and drew a bath with warm water.

Refreshed and changed into a soft long trouser with a top to match she left her room to explore the house which was now bathed in soft light from lamps in every room.

She found Ursula in the kitchen busy cooking.

"Thank you Ursula for unpacking and making me comfortable, I was very tired."

Smiling Ursula beckoned her to a chair she pulled out from the table.

"I saw that, are you feeling rested now?"

"Yes, I have never been a good traveller and my nerves exhaust me I'm afraid."

"Mr.Gerber will be down soon, he is, as you say, refreshing after work. We will have dinner in half an hour. The children have had their bath and will join us."

"Is there anything I can help you with?" Gail asked and Ursula smiled and pointed her to a lounge area where the children were sitting on the carpet watching television.

There was Veronica eleven, the eldest with a serious expression on her face. A petite girl with dark brown hair and hazel eyes that looked sad and interesting at the same time. Then there was Jacques who they called Jackie. He was more blond, with light brown eyes, and tall, for nine years of age, with a curious look on his face. Michael was six and had hazel eyes like his sister, with grey specks in them. His hair, was darker, nearly black, and his skin was more olive than his sister or brother.

He was smiling from ear to ear and that went straight to Gail's heart.

Gail got up and joined them to a warm welcome from all three.

"Hello Site" they all chimed. Gail sat on the sofa and it was not long before Michael sat next to her. He had a book with him that he was reading and Gail saw that it was in Afrikaans and was written in big fat letters around a story of three little pigs.

"Hou jy van hierdie storie?" she asked him and he answered "Ja."

"Nou toe", said Gail "lees vir my die storie."

This was how Anton saw them when he entered the room and he knew at that moment that he had made the right decision.

The meal was a pleasant affair. They all sat around the table with Anton at the head and the children flanking him. Anton asked them about their day and they each told him what they did that day.

After the meal Ursula went with the children to their rooms and Anton asked Gail to join him in the lounge for coffee. A tray was already laid out on a small table and he poured for both of them while in a pleasant manner he told her about his family. The reason they were in Austria and how his wife had died. Then it was Gail's turn to tell him more of her background. When her cup was empty she excused herself not wanting to overstay her visit and left.

She was uncertain where the bedrooms of the children were and did not want to be intrusive so she went to her own suite.

Gail saw that the part of the house where she was, was separated from the wing where the other bedrooms were, and realised that it was most likely a guest suite. This made her happy as she enjoyed watching television in the evenings and she would have felt uncomfortable had it been close to the family rooms. Tonight however, she would just relax and read a little to settle her mind after the stress of the past hours.

The book lay unopened on her lap as the events of the past few days were replayed in her head. Now and then a soft chuckle escaped her as she remembered how she nearly took a wrong flight after she had to go back to weigh her luggage. Well, she thought, not bad for a first time all on her own.

When the knock came on her door Gail was already dressed and her bed was neatly made up. Ursula had a tray packed with a small plate of Danish pastries and another with bacon and eggs just as she liked it. Well-done eggs and crispy bacon. She smiled at Ursula who placed the tray on a small table which Gail did not even notice the night before and uncovered the pot of tea kept warm with a knitted cover. This arrangement had been agreed on the night before as Gail said she did not want to be an overpowering presence with the children who may take some time to get used to her. After all grannies were not mommies and Gail wanted the children and their father and housekeeper not to feel that she was an intruder.

Chapter Four

BEFORE LEAVING SOUTH AFRICA Gail had her mobile telephone adjusted to international standard and she checked her mobile every so often but there was never a message. It was three days now since she left her home and not even one of her children had called to find out if she had arrived safely. Gail should have felt hurt but looking out of her window all she felt was exhilaration. It was almost as if a completely new life had presented itself and she smiled.

She found Ursula in the kitchen busy baking a cake and when she saw Gail she gave her a big smile.

"Come sit we have tea and nice cake."

"It does look wonderful, are you baking for something special?"

"Oh, ja! It is Veronicas birthday tomorrow, she will be having some friends over from school".

"Will she be twelve then?"

"Yes, already a young lady" Ursula said laughing.

"I am sorry, I did not know, I could have brought her something from South Africa" and here Gail paused "I wonder what she would have liked?"

"She has all she needs" Ursula said.

Gail wondered about that, and she made up her mind to spend some time with the children individually to get to know their likes and dislikes.

After tea and the most delicious chocolate cake that Gail had ever eaten she left Ursula in the kitchen to take a walk outside in the garden.

The children arrived home with the driver around three o'clock and found Gail waiting for them in the lounge.

"Hello kinders, hoe was julle dag?"

Little Michael ran to Gail and she picked him up on her lap and the other two plumped themselves down on the couch opposite.

The two older ones started talking without giving each other a chance and Gail gently lifted her hand and pointed to Veronica.

"Jy eerste Veronica en dan gee ons vir die ander 'n kans".

When Veronica stopped Gail pointed to Jackie and urged him to tell them about his day. Before little Michael had his chance he was fast asleep on Gail's lap. She sat for a while just savouring the moment of contentment before Ursula came to fetch him.

Veronica and changed into more comfortable clothes and joined Ursula in the kitchen for a light snack. Gail did not intrude in their time together.

She wanted to take no bonding time, away from anyone else, and felt she should only be a person when no other was available, much like a granny, and then she corrected herself. Not 'much like' but exactly as, and she smiled.

After all she did have experience in this department.

Evening after dinner found them all, except for Ursula, who was busy in the kitchen, spending time in the lounge. When Ursula called the children to prepare for bed, Gail stayed a short while longer where she and Anton exchanged some pleasantries from their days' events.

Gradually she found that Anton became more relaxed and occasionally he would allow a chuckle to escape his otherwise serious demeanour.

She did not overstay her time with him even though she would have liked to stay longer, but she did not want to be intrusive, and wanted to see the children before they slept.

She first stopped in Veronicas room to see if she could help her in any way, and found her sitting at her dressing table brushing her hair.

Gail went to her and took the brush from her and started lightly brushing her hair. Veronica closed her eyes and relaxed. "Thank you Site" she said, and then after a short silence, she spoke again "my mom used to do this for me."

Gail looked at Veronica in the mirror and a soft look came to her own eyes. "I used to do this for my daughter Sarah as well" she said and smiled at Veronica whose smile was reflected in the mirror.

After a few more strokes Gail put the brush down. She lightly kissed the top of Veronicas head and left quietly.

The next stop was at Jackie's door. The door was closed halfway and Gail lightly knocked and asked if she could go in, which she did after Jackie called her.

He was already in bed and had a book in his hand. Gail looked at the title and saw that he was reading a Hardy Boy adventure. She recognised the title from when she was a mere girl and smiled. "I see you like adventure".

"Yes, I want to be an adventure seeker one day. I would like to go to the Amazon and to the North Pole and even climb Mount Everest. What do you think Site, will I be able to do something like that?"

"One can do anything that one sets their mind to do but you must do it not just for the sake of saying you did it, but because it contributed some value to your own life."

Jackie took a little time to think about what Gail said and nodded.

"Adventure," Gail said "can be found in everyday life. Your father is an adventurer of sorts you know."

"But he only goes to the office" Jackie said.

"Well, in one day your father travels to many countries. Before eleven in the morning he will already have been in Japan and Switzerland and by three in the afternoon he had already visited with a gold mine in South Africa or been on a coffee plantation in Brazil."

Gail looked at Jackie and saw a puzzled look on his face as she walked to the door and after a light wave of her hand she made sure to leave the door half closed.

She looked in at Michael and saw that he was already asleep and realised she should have started with him, read him a story or just stayed with him for a while. Tomorrow, she promised herself, she would do that.

In her suite she checked her mobile to see if there were any messages. There were none and she felt sad once more. From her cupboard she took out her laptop and connected it to the plug in the wall. It was a very old computer and was given to her by another trustee while she was the chairperson at the estate where she lived.

She sometimes, but only sometimes, thought about those days. A good job had been done by transforming a barren landscape to lush gardens and bringing some kind of unity and closeness to the community that lived there. Well, her task was done there and now other trustees had that responsibility.

The program took long to load and she accepted that because she knew the computer was old just like her, so she waited patiently for the loading to be completed.

There it was, the colours beautiful and bright just like Africa, as the casino on line, opened it arms and welcomed Gail in.

Tonight she promised herself, she would only play blackjack and no more than her allotted amount allowed her for the night. When her money was doubled she closed the top and packed the computer away. Tomorrow she would play poker she promised herself.

The day started not as usual, if one can count the previous days that had passed as markers, but on a different note. Today, being a Saturday and no school was also the birthday party of Veronica, and a few friends were coming over to celebrate. Gail helped Ursula in the kitchen where they were packing platters of pastries and salted snacks. The table was set in the den and music was playing. An air of gaiety filled the room with all the friends laughing and dancing to the music. Jackie flitted in and out and little Michael sat in a corner watching. He had a small plate on his lap which was regularly replenished by Veronica.

Anton arrived late afternoon and made a brief visit to the den, then settled himself in the lounge, with the newspaper and soon little Michael found him there, and climbed on his lap where he fell asleep. Gail saw them like that and went to ask Ursula to take him to his room. She did not even attempt to take him herself knowing her limitations. Somehow, Gail thought to herself, as she followed Ursula to the room and covered Michael with a rug, that for once in a very long time, she was content.

Everything was like it was supposed to be. She went back to the lounge to chat to Anton still sitting in the same chair, with the newspaper now folded, and his eyes closed. When he heard her, he opened his eyes and smiled.

"Thank you Gail, for coming to us. You have made this family feel whole again."

"It is my privilege to be here Anton, it also makes me happy to be here."

Ursula brought a tray into the lounge and Gail saw that there were three cups, one for each of them, Ursula poured the tea and handed pastries around.

"Everything was very nicely done Ursula" Anton said. "Thank you for arranging it."

"Ag, I had help from Gail this time."

"Well then, thanks to both of you." He held his teacup like a salute and they both did the same.

With tea finished Ursula took the tray and Gail left as well.

In her room Gail stood for a while looking out of the window and when her mobile rang she was startled. With a quick dash towards it she pressed the green button without even looking at the screen to see who was calling.

"Hello!"

"Hi Mom! How are you?"

"My goodness, my child" she said "I thought you had completely forgotten me. How are you all?"

"We are all OK here, how was your flight?"

Gail was just about to remind him that, that event was nearly four days ago. but kept her remark back and said

"Everything was just fine thank you."

"Well, OK then mom, you keep well you hear."

She stared at the phone in her hand and shook her head. What a waste of a call, he may as well not have bothered. Tears welled up in her eyes and with a deep sigh she put the phone down.

Everything settled nicely. The children accepted Gail as a secondary mom and Anton seemed more relaxed and the best part was that Ursula became even more friendly and many mornings would find the two of them in he kitchen with a pot of tea and a plate of biscuits or cake between them.

Ursula started opening up about her family living in the midlands where her mother lived with her sister since her father passed away, and the two of them ran a small poultry farm. Ursula usually went to visit once a month. Gail told her about her children and what they did for a living and about their families. Ursula was surprised that Gail could leave all that behind and go to another country, and Gail told her of her lifetime longing to visit other places and never having been able to afford it, and what made her decide to do this at her advanced age, to achieve her dream.

It was a week and still no phone call from Gavin or Sarah. Well, Gail thought, lets see how long it will take before they want to know if their mother is still alive or not. Somehow it really did not matter quite so much any longer.

On a Monday Anton announced after dinner that he would be away on business for a few days and would be leaving the next morning. He said that Ursula would have a contact number if there was any emergency but he was happy to leave everything in their capable hands.

Gail felt as if she belonged and that she was actually an important part of a family and she smiled.

Ursula drove a small car and went into town regularly for supplies. So Gail was happy when she asked if she would like to go with. They stopped in the middle of a block of six shops and took a stroll first to the one end and then to the other as Ursula gave an introduction of all the shops and their wares. The weather being pleasant they decided to sit at an outside table of a small coffee shop where they ordered tea and scones. This came with homemade strawberry jam and fresh cream and looked delicious.

Gail was careful not to put any cream on her scone having been intolerant of this delicacy for the last few years, and instead put a generous helping of jam on, and she absolutely enjoyed it. Just maybe, she decided, she could try at the next opportunity to try the cream, and she smiled at that daring idea.

On the way back home, and Ursula having taken a different route, they passed a place selling scooters. On a sudden impulse Gail asked Ursula to stop and go back.

Scooters were displayed on a patch of grass in front of the shop. A bright yellow, a dark blue, and a light red one, were parked side by side.

Gail slowly walked around the machines and then sat on one. Her hands closed around the handles and she felt the wind blow through her hair as another idea took form. This, she decided would be her next goal.

Gail was deep in thought. Could she risk it? Would she be able to manage the machine? Could she afford it? The answer to all three questions was a definite NO! But the nagging idea never left her.

That evening after dinner, Ursula joined Gail and he children in the lounge. Veronica took a game of scrabble from the cupboard that stretched across the whole wall, and soon they were all laughing and having fun.

When Anton returned home from his business trip he once again felt he had made a good decision to hire a granny for his family. He saw the children bloom and even Ursula looked happier.

Gail spent more and more time with the children and when Veronica came home with a notice inviting parents to an evening where parents and teachers could discuss their progress, Anton asked Gail if she would mind to go as he had another appointment that he could not change. Ursula said she would take her but would go back for her as she had someone she had to visit, so early evening saw the two of them on their way to the school in Ursula's small car.

Gail had a list of teacher's names and classroom numbers in her hand when she entered the school building. It was very old and she saw there were no creepers on the walls and the large stones that were used had a soft pink tone to them. She took in the well kept gardens and saw the people arriving, greeting each other, as if they knew them for a long time.

She marvelled at the thought that she was actually there. An air of unreality and excitement was like a bubbling stream running through her veins.

The school catered for scholars from pre-school to matriculation, or whatever they called it there, and had more that a thousand scholars.

With a light step she walked into the entrance where she found the class numbers with arrows pointing to the respective areas. Her first stop on her list was to Jackie's teacher where she found a few people already waiting to talk to the teacher. Not being able to stand for long with her knees weakened by arthritis, Gail slid behind a desk and waited her turn.

It was as if the years rolled back and she was in school again. The feeling made her smile as she watched the teacher explaining to the parents about their children and their progress. When it was her turn she held out her hand to introduce herself.

"Oh, the teacher said, I am happy to meet Jackie's granny. He speaks often about you."

Gail was surprised but kept her thoughts to herself and smiled but the feeling of belonging was like a warm cloak around her shoulders.

The progress report was satisfactory and she thanked the teacher and went to the next one. There were many parents waiting and Gail decided to go to the next teacher and then come back.

Walking along the corridor she thought back to the days not of her childhood but to the time when she worked as administrative assistant in a primary school where her own children attended. She always regarded those years as the happiest in her past life.

When she pulled her thoughts back to the present she saw that she had gone too far and turned back.

Miss Banks, Michael's teacher was just saying goodbye to parents and Gail was next, so she stood and waited.

"Good evening, you must be Michael's gran?"

Surprised Gail said "Yes, how did you know?"

Miss Banks smiled and Gail saw why Michael spoke so much about his teacher. Her manner and soft spoken voice was pleasant to listen to. It was tinged with a slight lilt and obvious to Gail that she was not from the area.

"I have spoken to all the other parents and it was only Michael's name that was not ticked off on my list."

Five minutes passed quickly with Miss Banks telling Gail about Michael's progress and with a start Gail realised that she still had to go back to Veronica's teacher. She quickly made her apologies and rushed out of the room. Just in time it was, as the last parent left and Gail was next. After introducing herself Mrs Grader gave her Veronica's progress report and after thanking her Gail was turning to leave when Mrs Grader said "Veronica is a very unhappy girl, you know."

"I am sorry" Gail said "I did not know it was so noticeable, do you think it has gotten worse lately?" Maybe Veronica felt she, Gail was an intrusion. The feeling of well-being that was prominent earlier disappeared like a deflated balloon.

"Well" Mrs Grader said "I think she has been feeling better over the past few weeks."

Gail's heart gave a flutter of relief and she realised again like so many times before that a state of happiness was held by a fragile thread that frayed easily.

"Thank you, Mrs Grader, I hope that she will improve steadily. Please feel free to contact me at any time if you feel you need to."

"I certainly will" Mrs Grader said and Gail left.

Ursula was waiting for her when she left the building and they chatted about their evening. By the time they arrived home the children having already had their bath was waiting in the lounge for them.

Gail went to each one and hugged them.

"Well done to all of you, your father will surely be happy."

The children grinned clearly relieved.

"Tonight it is Veronica's turn to read." Gail said as she settled on the couch next to Michael.

Veronica took the book that they were reading from each night, from the shelf and started to read.

This was an evening event that Gail had quickly introduced. One night Veronica would read and the next night was Jackie's turn. Michael just listened and was usually asleep within minutes when Ursula would carry him to his bed.

Chapter Five

O N A CLEAR SUNNY morning Ursula took Gail to collect the yellow scooter that was waiting for her.

For two weeks one of the young assistants working at the agency had taken Gail out to teach her how to ride. Gail remembered the first time she got on to the scooter and started it. It was downright scary to say the least. She never thought she would manage but after a few attempts it was easy. The roads around the town were not busy and Gail knew she would enjoy this new experience.

Smiling she produced her licence to the owner of the shop and he made a copy and then put it into a file which he kept on a shelf behind the counter. He handed her the keys and the receipt for payment and shook her hand wishing her well with her new purchase.

Ursula waited long enough to make sure that Gail was on her way before following her to the coffee shop. The two of them lifted their cups in a salute to the yellow scooter parked next to the kerb directly in front of the coffee shop.

Gail was happy, her heart was filled with excitement and a feeling of wellbeing enveloped her. She was a new person, one with a purpose, one with plans, one filled with happiness. A smile was permanently etched on her face.

The countryside became like a book opening a new page each day as Gail flitted from one spot to another. When she passed people walking, or riding, she would wave and they would wave back. Yes! Life was good.

Evenings before bathing Gail would take out her laptop and connect the cables then check her e-mail messages which were not usually very fruitful.

But on this particular night, she saw with some surprise, that there were more than usual. Gail never liked this form of communication, as you never knew what could pop up, but it was the way things were done these days so she accepted that, after all, it was amazing how one could chat in this way. She scrolled down each message and deleted the junk mail as she went on. The first real message was from her youngest son Gavin.

"Hi Mom. How are things there? We are all well but missing you."

Smiling Gail thought how her life had changed. Instead of sitting at home hoping for some kind of gesture to acknowledge her, she was in this wonderful place, which was becoming as if she was always supposed to be here.

Her answer took nearly the whole page as she told him about her new scooter and where she had been with it. When she clicked the send button she felt sad for a moment just thinking of her son so far away.

School holidays were approaching and Anton told Gail that the family would be spending some time in the city of Vienna and that would include her as well.

"We always took the children to see the great theatres and galleries. Shame to not let them get to know the country that they are currently living in."

A far away look in his eyes as he spoke showed the pain of the loss he felt with his wife's passing. Gail, although she had also loved her life mate, instinctively knew it was different. He was still young, a man in his prime and he must surely miss a companion.

To say that Gail was excited would be a gross understatement. She was near to tears just thinking about the dream that would be enfolding shortly. She was also happy that it meant the children would have more time with their father. Gail knew that he cared for them but at the same time ached for them not having a mother. She saw this all in his eyes when he watched them in the evenings playing their games.

"Ursula" Gail said the next morning in the kitchen while they were having breakfast "what clothes should I take?"

"Comfortable shoes for walking. A smart dress for the theatre. No pants!"

"Oh dear!" Gail said. "I wonder if I should look for something special in town?"

"No, don't do that. Much better to shop in Vienna."

"Of course, you are right as always."

She wished that Ursula was coming as well but knew that this was also the time when Ursula would take leave and visit her family.

The next few days were filled with a flurry of selecting clothes for the children and making sure that the clothes still fitted them. They grew so fast she thought, while Ursula helped her with the task. A list was nearby where Ursula was writing all the things down that they needed.

Gail and the children would make shopping a priority when they were in Vienna.

Excitement was in the air. The children were more talkative and Gail felt like a small child as she checked and re-checked the list of things to take with. All other thoughts took a backseat as she went through the daily routine on auto pilot.

Ursula was also looking forward to her trip and the last day before leaving saw them ticking lists of their own.

Ursula took care of Anton's luggage, and packed all the things he left out on his bed.

Finally they were ready. The children dressed for the trip were waiting in the lounge.

The evening before, Gail had parked her yellow scooter in the garage where it would be safer and after she and the children left with the driver Ursula would lock everything up. The house was to be closed until two days before their return, when Ursula would be back to get things ready for them.

The trip to the airport was without Anton, who would meet them there.

Gail was nervous. She hoped that she had everything although she knew Ursula had made sure of that. She kept this nervous feeling hidden from the children and instead smiled at them as the car sped along with her and Veronica and little Michael in the back with Jackie upfront with the driver.

Chapter Six

I T WAS VERONICA THAT led them into the airport. This was a trip they had made before and she knew what had to be done. Gail followed with the two boys and then they soon saw Anton. Relief washed over Gail and she was amazed how she had come to rely on this man. She felt at times hat he was her son. This was of course not true but the thought was not uncomfortable.

Gail was not surprised when they were shown to their seats in the business class area of the aircraft knowing that she somehow expected it. They settled in with Veronica and little Michael beside Gail while Jackie sat with his father and they were already chatting about the aircraft.

Earlier Gail had of course taken her tablet to make travelling more bearable and it also helped her nervousness. She had also crushed a half and stirred it in the cool drink she had given Michael before they left. She did this because Ursula told her Michael always took ill when travelling. Gail hoped the tablet would work for him as it did for her.

Oh! What joy, was the feeling that swept over her as she gazed out of her window from her suite at the hotel. The beauty of the city that stretched out before her made her heart beat faster. She still found it difficult to believe that she was actually in Vienna.

Ever since she read all those novels of bygone ages with princes and Tzars and all their balls it was like a dream that had come true.

Gail turned around when Veronica called her. "Site what time are we meeting Dad?"

"We still have half an hour" was her reply "so you can finish your letter."

Veronica was writing to a friend and wanted to post the letter on their way.

Their suite in the hotel consisted of three bedrooms, two bathrooms and a lounge and Gail and the children settled in very nicely while Anton had a suite further along the passage with two rooms, bathroom and lounge.

Anton had business meetings to attend to, and he had arranged his schedule with Gail during their flight. She and the children would have ample free time to see the sights and do some shopping. They were in Vienna for a week and then he would hire a car, and take time with them to explore other smaller towns on their route to West Germany where he also had meetings.

The children were in high spirits and chatted away waiting in the lobby of the hotel where Anton met them. They ran to him and he hugged them all together.

He looked relaxed as they walked out of the door with Gail behind, walking as if on a cloud, looking at everything around her. She saw only beauty. The restaurant he took them to was not very far so they walked the distance. They passed stylish shops with hardly anything in their windows. One shop had only one scarf displayed which was draped on a Victorian upholstered chair. Gail knew that the price tag on the scarf must be high.

The next day and every other one that followed made her body feel like a sponge soaking up all the sights and the people, the architecture and shop windows, filled with extraordinary things. Days went quickly as they explored the city. The children had been there before and it was Jackie who led the way most days with Veronica and little Michael sometimes lagging behind. Soon, Gail thought, Jackie would be a young man and she wondered if she would be around to see that. She hoped so.

Evenings were spent with Anton taking them to grand restaurants and the theatre which so impressed Gail that she thought she was dreaming.

Gail had putt off her mobile phone most of the time and this did not seem to be a problem as there were no messages from anyone, no children and no friends. Funny she thought, this did not bother her at all. She felt completely detached from her previous world.

Too soon the week was over and the suitcases packed into a minibus that Anton hired complete with a driver.

Excited laughter was contagious in the vehicle and once outside the city limits they all sang along, even the driver.

Gail knew this was the kind of life she had dreamed of and one she never thought she would get the opportunity to participate in. Happy was what she was, yes, very happy indeed. Best of all was that she saw Anton was more relaxed and not so serious.

They stopped for tea in a small village where they all had fresh scones with delicious homemade strawberry jam and fresh cream in little bowls.

Late afternoon they stopped again for lunch.

From the time they had set off in the morning to this late afternoon Gail noticed a difference in the people of the towns where they stopped for refreshment.

Their manner was different, less friendly though courteous. The food was excellent and always well presented. Gail could see that the children were tired and when they finally stopped at their hotel she was as happy as they were and she gently woke little Michael who was asleep with his head on her lap.

A light drizzle fell the next morning and spirits were dampened it was clear that the children did not enjoy being confined in a vehicle all day. Long silences left empty spaces as each were locked in their own thoughts. Gail found herself thinking of her own children left behind and a longing feeling made her sad. She was sure that Anton was probably also thinking of his late wife and who knows the children may also be thinking along those lines. She was glad when they stopped for morning tea at a small coffee shop.

When they got into the vehicle again the driver handed out small blankets to cover their legs. The light drizzle continued and before long they were all dozing off.

When they stopped for a late lunch Gail awoke with a start and was amazed that she had slept for more than two hours. The children were also crabby and wished that they had already reached their destination.

Gail was determined to not fall asleep again while driving. She hated this feeling of being enveloped in cotton wool so once in the vehicle and settled before starting the final lap of the day, she announced that they would play a game of 'I spy'.

At first there was not much enthusiasm but the feeling changed as the game proceeded and very soon they were all involved, even the driver.

Each one had a turn to start a new game and before long they stopped at their hotel. A cosy family establishment was set at the foot of a hill with tall pine trees circling the estate. Big oak carved doors stood open waiting for visitors.

Inside the air was comfortably warm and Gail saw a giant fireplace where logs were smouldering. A delicious smell of meat roasting wafted in the air. It was a place of relaxation and cosiness and Gail felt immediately at home.

In the dining room she sat with the children while Anton sat with the driver on another table where the owner of the hotel joined them.

There were six other people in the dining room and he waiter put large beer glasses in front of Anton and the driver as well as the other guests.

He brought one for Gail as well but she declined and before long the sounds of joking and laughter was bouncing from wall to wall. A feeling of happiness had brushed away the low spirits and the children were chatting while Gail watched with a smile.

Afterwards Gail and the children gathered in the lounge where the fire was still going strong with fresh logs stacked on the coals. Jackie and Veronica sat on the carpet in front of the fire and little Michael sat next to Gail on a comfortable couch.

'This is our Ghost Time.'

The children looked at Gail in anticipation as she had promised them earlier while still driving that the hour after dinner would be called the 'Spooky Hour' where each evening one of them would have to tell a ghost story. This turned out to be most enjoyable although it left little Michael with big eyes and clinging to Gail.

Chapter Seven

AFTER A GOOD NIGHT'S sleep and a hearty breakfast the group piled into the vehicle.

There was still a light drizzle and grey skies loomed overhead. The driver handed them blankets again to put over their knees.

It took a while for the heating system to warm the inside of the vehicle but once it was warmed up they were comfortable.

Thankfully they did not have far too go for their final destination and Gail looked out of the window at the passing countryside. The whole scene had changed from the time they left Austria. Dour and uninteresting farmsteads caused no exciting flutters to her heart and she was happy that their stay would not be long in Germany. She was already looking forward to their onward journey to Switzerland where they would be staying for four days before flying home.

This thought rejuvenated her spirit as she fantasised racing down a steep slope covered with snow. Would she be able to actually do it? Well, she would try anyway she thought.

"What are you thinking about Site?' Michael asked looking up at her.

Gail put her arm around him and hugged his little body to her chest.

"I am thinking about Switzerland. Do you think we will be able to ski?'

'Of course we will Site' Veronica answered. 'We always do. I will show you how.'

'Well, I take that as a promise.' Gail said. 'So let me go first with I spy?'

"I spy with my little eye something that is round, with red dots."

'I know what it is' Jackie said 'it is a ladybird.'

Gail had seen this little creature on the inside of the front window and wondered if anyone else had also seen it.

'Of course you are right Jackie.' Now it was his turn.

The road became wider as they sped along and then there were cars all around them. Gail was amazed at the sudden change of scene and the children also sat bolt upright looking out of the windows.

'Wow' Jackie said excitedly. 'Dad what is that car there?' Pointing to a strange looking car riding alongside of them.

Anton turned hid head and went into the make of it with enthusiasm and then their conversation became engrossed at all the different shapes and sizes of the vehicles. There were really small ones and some that were very large. Gail also looked at the rows of cars like giant pythons sliding, or so it seemed, along the multi lanes. So this is the autobahn she thought. What a truly incredible sight.

The driver weaved in and out of the traffic and then took a road to the left and they were suddenly in the city.

There were people everywhere and Gail felt an increase in the tempo and this seemed to increase by the second.

Now for the first time since they had left their home in Austria did she feel excitement bubbling through her body. The feeling made her heady and she took a few deep breaths to calm herself.

Barely three months have passed since her journey from South Africa and her new life filled her with a zest for more. She knew she was truly alive and said a silent prayer for being able to be there.

When the driver stopped in front of the hotel the children were unable to keep their excitement in check and were out of the vehicle before the driver could open the doors. They gathered in a group on the sidewalk and could hardly wait for their father who put a restraining hand on their shoulders when he joined them.

Excitedly the children ran ahead to their suite with the porter.

Gail smiled and enjoyed their exuberance. She could not help feeling that the children were indeed feeling more relaxed than when she had first come to stay with them. She also felt grateful for the opportunity to be part of their family circle. They had accepted her in the role of grandmother as if she was just that.

After a very comforting lunch in the dining room they could not wait to explore the city.

Anton was not be joining them for their exploration but he gave Gail a list of nearby places to visit. So with little Michael's hand held tight in her own they followed Veronica and Jackie who seemed to know where they were going.

'Site can we please, please go to the movies tonight?'

Jackie had asked about going to a movie long before the family even left Austria and had to be content to wait. Now in this fast moving city there was a movie theatre not far from the hotel where they were staying.

'Go and see what time there will be a show Jackie. Be careful don't rush.'

He quickly walked to see the show times displayed on a board and Veronica followed him.

There was a show starting in fifteen minutes and after a short discussion with the children Gail bought their tickets. Although the dialogue would be in German with English subtitles they were not concerned about it.

The queue was not long at the popcorn counter and they were soon settled in their seats. Little Michael soon fell asleep where he sat and Gail lifted him on to her lap where he lay in her arm. She was happy and knew the children were as well. The movie was too exciting for Gail with cars chasing around but she knew Jackie and Veronica was enjoying it so she let her mind wander thinking of her own family so far away. Did they even miss her?

Michael woke up shortly before the movie ended and they went back to the hotel where Anton was already waiting. They joined him in the lounge and then went to their suite to freshen before he took them out for dinner.

The night scene they rode into was of people, lights and noise. The children were clearly excited and Gail saw Anton smiling. Life was good!

The restaurant was quite informal and pleasant as was the food and service. Tired of their long day they went to bed as soon as they got back to the hotel. Anton had business meetings the next day and Gail had her list of places to take the children to.

Once the children were all settled in bed Gail took out her laptop. She had not used this for some time and called up her mailbox. Mostly junk mail which was immediately discarded, and left only one message from her son Jake. Oh well! She thought, at least one of them did spare her a thought as she opened it

'Hi Mom, how are you? We are all OK but miss you.'

Gail doubted that but typed a reply.

'Vienna was great! Germany is very exciting. Will be here three days to see sights then off to Switzerland. Give my love to all. Mom.' Then she clicked on send. That's that then, she thought, let them see I am not just sitting at home. She was going to close the laptop but decided to go on line and play some roulette. After a short while playing she upped her bet and had a particular good win on number twenty-four, her most favourite number, and clicked on cashier to transfer the money to her account. Yes! Life is good!

Three days went by in a flash finding them each evening tired and content and when the luggage was packed into the vehicle and they were settled in, it was with some sadness and backward glances that they left the city.

Chapter Eight

WHEN THE CAR LEFT the city limits the landscape changed and an air of excitement made Gail feel giddy. The children were chatting to each other while Anton was talking to the driver. No-one took much notice of Gail and she was letting her thoughts drift along. Her arrival seemed so long ago but in fact only three months had passed. So much had happened during that time that she had to look into a mirror to remind her who she really was. The bored unhappy old woman who felt unloved and uncared for had changed into this glowing happy person. It was a feeling she hoped would continue for a long time. So deep in thought she was that Anton had to call her twice before she heard him

'Gail, Gail . . .'

He smiled at her when she looked at him.

'We will be stopping shortly for some refreshment and will get a hamper for the road ahead. The next stretch will be long with nowhere to stop.'

'OK' Gail said and wondered what they would find at their stop.

A short while later they stopped at a roadside café and coffee shop.

They all climbed out to go to the toilet and then went inside. Anton took a basket and Gail walked with him as they selected items to take with. Gail was surprised to see the lovely homemade breads and cakes and pickled jars on display and they soon had a collection of food that she thought would be suitable.

They were all in high spirits when they got into the vehicle carrying the packets.

An hour later they stopped at a demarcated roadside site. Stone benches and a table were placed in a circle and Gail spread the food out so each one could help themselves to the delicious bread, cheese, cold meat and fruit juice.

It felt like a proper picnic and although the air was cold nobody seemed to mind. When they finished their meal they packed what was left back into the packets and deposited the empty cartons in the bin provided before setting off again. Three hours later they stopped and had the rest of the food and it was early evening when they arrived at their destination.

The building was dimly lit and looked very quiet but a door was opened as soon as the vehicle stopped, spreading light onto the wide veranda.

Inside a cosy fire warmed the air and warm drinks were poured from a tall thermos. The hot chocolate felt like velvet to Gail and she wrapped her hands around the mug to warm them.

Although the drive was comfortable they were all tired and cranky and after a wholesome dinner of thick soup and lamb stew they retired.

'Site, Site!' Little Michael was shouting for Gail to wake up. 'Come and see.' Gail got out of her bed and followed him to the window. There outside were three horses with their riders who stood in a small group together.

'Please Site, can we ride on the horses?' He was pleading and now Veronica and Jackie had also joined them.

'Jackie, run down and ask the riders if we can, while we get dressed.'

Jackie was outside in a flash. The children loved riding horses and Gail knew they missed this while away. She got dressed in a hurry and then helped Michael. Veronica was waiting for them downstairs when Jackie came walking towards them.

'Only two of us can go at a time, they need to have a rider along. Can I please go first?'

Gail looked at him still in his pyjamas and shook her head. 'You first go and dress Jackie. Let Veronica and Michael go then you can have a turn when they come back. He was disappointed but realised she was right and left to change.

Veronica and Michael were helped onto the horses, and together with a rider set off.

Jackie did not take long to dress and was waiting with Gail for them to return. Gail watched them, remembering when she was a young girl, and how she rode a horse on her grandfathers' farm. On impulse she found herself walking to the two riders standing nearby.

When the trio returned it was not only Jackie getting on to a horse but Gail as well. A rider helped her into the saddle. She was nervous sitting so high and wondered whatever made her make such a rash decision. What was she thinking? Surely she should know better than to think like a teenager, and for a fleeting moment, she considered getting off, but found herself unable to do so, and instead took three deep breaths and took the reins.

She held them loosely in her hand like she was told so long ago.

They started off at a slow pace and Gail relaxed a little thinking it was not so bad after all. When the pace was increased to a trot, she was ready for it.

Exhilarated on their return she found Anton waiting with the children. A smile and a shake of his head greeted her. Her legs felt like rubber as she walked slowly but steadily with them to have breakfast.

To say she surprised herself, would be a gross understatement, and she made up her mind to send an e-mail to her own children that evening, to tell them about her day, while a smile played on her lips.

A hearty breakfast and they were on their way again. It was getting colder and they all had their little blankets covering their legs. The journey would take a few hours and before long little Michael fell asleep resting his head on her lap.

Anton was in conversation with Jackie and now and again Veronica would chip in. Gail watched and was happy for them. A bond that had been severed by grief was slowly getting stronger again. Her eyes closed and she dozed off. When Michael stirred she awoke just in time to see them pulling up to a hotel. The building was surrounded by tall fir trees and pots of geraniums gave a splash of colour. The hotel seemed almost translucent with the weak rays of the sun glinting on it. Almost like a fairy castle she thought, as a porter opened the car door to help them out.

They would be here for three days while Anton was going to be in the city having meetings. These were the last few days before they flew back home. When Gail explored the hotel with the children after they had refreshed in their suite, she knew why Anton had chosen it instead of the city. There was a fully equipped gym and hot springs bubbled in an enclosed conservatory sending up steam which clouded the vast windows.

They did not even look further, and Gail asked an attendant to help them. Soon they were all in swimming costumes with caps on their heads and splashing in the warm water. Jackie and Veronica were in the deeper water while Gail and Michael played in the shallow area.

They had a lot of fun and enjoyed themselves tremendously.

An attendant brought them warm robes and they all sat around a table drinking hot chocolate and swam again before returning to their rooms to change for lunch. They were famished when they arrived in the dining room and eagerly ate their food.

With dinner over they went to the lounge where games were being set up for the residents to play. Board games of scrabble and monopoly and cards at another table. At the lower end of the room carpet bowls were laid out ready for play. Tickets were on sale from a young man sitting at a small table at the entrance. A clipped batch entitled one to five games and prizes were to be drawn later. Fun and laughter was the order of the evening and they all enjoyed themselves. When prize time came Veronica won a full body massage at their health centre and Jackie a jet-ski ride on the nearby frozen lake. Gail and little Michael won no prizes.

Happy, content and ready for bed after the enjoyment of the day, Gail settled them in bed, and they fell asleep almost instantly.

Gail sat at the window in her room, with the curtains drawn back, staring at the sky where the stars shone like polished gold. The beauty filled her heart with such intensity, she thought it might burst. Here she was, she thought, an old woman who spent countless hours alone and giving way to tears of self pity waiting for her telephone to ring so she could hear a familiar voice, in this beautiful place. Here happiness and laughter made her a part of something again. She closed the curtains and took out her laptop from the cupboard and linked it up. First she checked her e-mail messages. There were two from her children besides the junk mail which she first deleted.

'Hi Mom.' From Gavin her youngest child. 'Sounds like you are having a ball.

We are all OK and send you our love. Love you lots Gavin.'

The second message was from Jake, her eldest 'Gee Mom, just don't overdo things, give yourself a rest.' If only he knew how she hated taking a rest. That was all she ever did at home, rest and read, how boring. With relish she started tapping away on the keyboard.

'Arrived today, in Switzerland. Beautiful hotel in a big estate, pine trees around it. Spent the afternoon in hot springs with the children and had an evening of games in the lounge. Children are already sleeping after a hectic day and I will retire soon. Tomorrow we have something special planned and will let you know how it goes.' Here she paused a while. It was all very well to tell them about her goings on, but what about them, are they OK?

Gail was enjoying her stay very much but the attraction of family ties stretched over mountains and oceans and so she let her guard down just a little.

'So nice to hear from you, are you really all well. How are things at work and home? I think of you all every day and hope you do the same for me. Love you always. Mom.'

Gail copied it to all three her children, even though only two had sent her mail. She closed her e-mail program and clicked on her on-line betting key. More than an hour went by and she was enjoying herself, winning a total of five hundred rand, and decided to call it a day. She was going to press the exit key, but instead, clicked on progressive games on the panel. She chose slots. When the game came on the screen she saw that there was a progressive amount of three hundred and forty thousand rand.

The currency was in South African rand, because her host was in South Africa. Gail had kept her same details when she left the country and planned to keep it that way. She started playing and before long her five hundred rand had shrunk to three hundred rand. Well, she thought, only another hundred more, and then she would pack it in.

Before she knew it her balance was down to sixty rand over her initial two hundred rand and this quickly shrunk to forty, and Gail wondered why it was so difficult to stop. She had increased her two hundred rand to five hundred and now she had lost her winnings yet again, she just never learned. As she pressed the last press before reaching the reserved two hundred rand, the screen suddenly lit up and stars burst all over, and the word 'jackpot' flashed on and off.

The sudden flash startled her, and she felt her heart pump faster, while at the same time, she held her breath in, as she waited for the payout to appear. Three hundred and forty-six thousand rand, was the amount that kept flashing. Could this really be happening she thought, maybe it is just a dream.

But no, another message came on the screen. 'Congratulations Gail you have won the progressive jackpot amounting to three hundred and forty-six thousand rand, would you like to go to cashier?'

'Yes' Gail clicked on cashier, and gave her credit card details, and then logged off. She was sure that it was only a dream and that she would go on line tomorrow to find that she still only had the two hundred rand in her account.

After packing away the laptop, she ran a warm bath. She knew she would have difficulty sleeping that night, so after making sure the children were all safe asleep, she bit off a three quarter of her sleeping tablet. She knew her usual half would not be enough with all the excitement rushing through her veins.

Early the next morning, Veronica woke Gail, anxious to make an appointment for her body massage. Jackie was soon there as well, wanting to know about his ski run. Little Michael climbed on her bed and asked what he could do, and all Gail wanted to do was to check her bank account. She knew she would have no time for herself till much later.

The jet-ski was scheduled for after breakfast and they left Jackie in the hands of the instructor, while Gail and Michael went with Veronica, to the health centre. She made sure as she sat nearby that she could see Veronica at all times. After all that is what grannies did, watched over their grand children. Little Michael was playing at her feet with a set of dinky cars they had bought in Germany. He loved to play with them and it kept him busy for hours. Also on the floor was the small suitcase she had bought for him to carry his cars in. She looked at him lovingly as she went back in thought to the time when her own children were small and she had sat like now watching them, a gentle smile played on her lips.

Chapter Nine

A SOFT GLOW MADE THE house seem surreal when the party arrived back from their holiday and Gail marvelled at the scene as she had done so many times before. It really was such a pleasant scene and the house made one feel welcome from the start. The children were excited to be back and ran to their rooms. Ursula hugged Gail in a warm greeting and asked how the trip had been. 'Yes' Gail said 'It was wonderful, and it is even more wonderful to be home.'

A welcoming aroma wafted in from the kitchen where a feast was in the making. Gail went to refresh herself and then joined Ursula in the kitchen where the finishing touches for the homecoming meal was completed.

Chatter and laughter filled the room where they all sat at the table as the children told Ursula of their holiday. Anton smiled but did not enter into the conversation leaving the children to talk about their trip. The meal was outstanding and Gail enjoyed every dish that Ursula had made. There was just nothing that she could compare it with in all the places that they had been to. Gail also did not actively participate in the conversation and left the children to share their stories with Ursula.

She noticed that Anton said very little but did not let it worry her. She was too content to think of anyone at that moment.

When dinner was over they all relaxed in the lounge chatting about their holiday and then Ursula told them about her visit to her own family. Later she brought them all a hot drink and sent them to bed.

School was still closed for the next two days, so the children had a chance to sleep late the next morning.

Gail had had an early breakfast with Ursula and was busy washing her scooter outside on the grass when Jackie came to her.

'Site, are you going to go for a ride?'

'Absolutely, Jackie, do you want to come with?'

'No, not this time, but you must enjoy it.' Gail thought he would leave her to finish but then he spoke again. 'Site, I want you to know that it was lovely to go away with you. I hope we can do it again at some time.'

Gail put the wet cloth in the bucket and went to Jackie and held him to her chest. He was nearly as tall as she was, and she kissed him on the top of his head. 'I am the lucky one Jackie you make a huge difference to my life. I want you to always remember that, no matter how old you are.' Then she let him go and carried on with her scooter. She did not look at him afraid that he may see the tears in her eyes, so instead she busied herself until he walked away.

She could hardly wait to take a ride through the streets thinking how she missed her little friend. After putting on her helmet she rode out of the driveway. It was more than an hour later that she returned. Ursula had tea ready and Gail and the children all sat around the kitchen table jabbering away. Anton left for work early and they would see him at dinner. 'What bliss' Gail thought as she looked at the faces surrounding her 'what happiness.'

Weeks turned into months, and then into years, as the children grew and achieved at school.

All this changed the week before their third Christmas together.

Jackie would turn fourteen early in January, and Veronica had turned sixteen in the November past. Little Michael was eight and looked tall for his age although Gail still thought of him as 'little'.

They were gathered in the lounge one evening while Ursula was still in the kitchen when Anton announced that he had something to tell them.

They looked expectantly at him, all three children, and Gail felt a sudden twinge in her heart. She instinctively knew their little group would not be together for long. The feeling made her heart constrict and she steeled herself for the words that she knew would come.

'I have met a wonderful woman.'

Looking at his face Gail saw his eyes shine as he spoke of her.

'I have asked her to marry me and she accepted. We will be married on February the second.'

Veronica first spoke 'I am happy for you Daddy, you have been alone far too long.'

'Will she like us?' Jackie asked and little Michael, who was not so little anymore, got up to sit at his fathers feet and asked 'when will we meet her Daddy?'

Gail sat very quietly and drank in the scene before her. She knew she would have to file all these special moments in a place in her heart where she could take it out from time to time to bask in.

When Gail joined Ursula in the kitchen the next morning she knew that Anton had also spoken to Ursula. Her manner was quiet and she hardly smiled. The children also had many questions when they arrived from school but Gail had no answers and neither did Ursula.

They would be meeting their father's fiancé on Saturday. He was going to bring her home to introduce her to his family.

Ursula cleaned the house with a determination till everything shone and then baked some biscuits and two of her delicious cakes, while Gail went into a detached mode. In her mind a list of things to do was taking shape. Jackie had been riding her scooter in the afternoons and even Veronica sometimes rode around in the driveway. She decided that she would leave her trusty friend with the children, after all she thought, they enjoyed using it.

The ad on the internet took much more time to plan. If she was going to make a change where would she want to go?

She had over the years gone to several countries with Anton and the children and could not make up her mind where she would like to be.

She knew for certain that she had to go and it was just a question of where to go to. She also knew that her timing had to be just right. She wanted to be there for the children when they needed her most but she would have to be gone before the wedding took place. There was no way she could be there when the new wife arrived. Ursula would stay on, she knew, because Anton did not want his wife to be concerned with the upkeep of the house and looking after the children, but Gail was a different kettle of fish altogether. She had discussed this with Anton and he agreed with her.

A package of retirement was discussed and Gail was surprised at the generosity of it. She would not have to be concerned about money for a very long time and this gave her a sense of security. She did after all still have some money in the bank from her winnings.

A list of countries was made which she kept next to her laptop and every evening she chose one to explore on the internet. She had e-mailed her children to tell them that she would be leaving after Christmas and would let them know where she was going at a later date.

Saturday came and the visit was actually quite pleasant. Nicole was an attractive woman of slight build and a gentleness about her. Gail liked her and so it seemed did Ursula. The children were shy and did not have much to say and Gail knew that they would have questions later when they were alone.

All three came to her room where she was busy checking her e-mails that evening. They sat on the bed and the questions started.

'Do you think she will like us?' Veronica asked. Gail saw they were eagerly waiting for her answer.

'I do believe she will do, there is nothing about you that anyone cannot like.'

'Do you think she also has children?' Michael asked. 'No, I know she has no children, your father told me so.'

'Will you be staying with us Site?'

'No Jackie, I will be leaving soon after Christmas.'

'We don't want you to leave Site.' Michael went to Gail and hugged her.

'I will never be away from you all. Look, I am going to make sure you have an e-mail set up, and we will send letters to each other. Would you like to do that?'

Veronica and Jackie had both used Gail's laptop some evenings to do research work for school and watched her answering her mail so they knew how to use it.

They were happy with her answer and she promised that she would set up their link in the next week. Ursula took Gail to town to buy a computer for the children. She dropped Gail at the computer shop while she did some errands and would return a bit later.

Gail settled on a slimmer version of her own computer which was quite old. She liked the sleek look and it was also much more technically up to date. She was amazed that she could actually converse with the assistant about the specs all in German. She had definitely grown in self confidence and was not that unsure old woman that she thought she was. It was while she was talking to the assistant that she knew where she wanted to go to and a path suddenly opened clear in her mind.

She felt sure about her decision and was excited. She would send off an advert that same night. On the spur of the moment she bought not one but two laptop computers. The children were nearly adults she reasoned and Veronica and Jackie should each have their own. As she walked out of the shop another thought struck her. What about Michael? Should she get him one as well? She turned around and went back into the shop.

Anton was seldom at home in the evenings like he used to be and after dinner Gail helped the children to link up their computers. She made them promise not to abuse the services provided and explained about the dangers that lurked within them and not to spend too much time at their computer and alone in their rooms. She wanted them to always make time for each other and to communicate in a friendly and supportive manner. She also asked them to make an effort to make their fathers wife feel at home and to give her a chance to get to know them better. She explained that as this woman did not have any children of her own she would need all the help they could give her. After all, they wanted their father to be happy and then they in turn would be happy.

The ad she sent was short 'Granny for hire, experienced with children young and old. No domestic duties included. Fluent in English and Afrikaans.' Gail checked the list that 'Google' had given and she selected three names all sounding westernised. Before she pressed enter she looked at the list again and selected another two, both sounding Asian then she pressed enter and logged off. All she could do now was wait.

Christmas was a family affair with Anton's fiancé joining them in the celebration as well as Ursula who had baked the most delicious cakes and biscuits. A feast of turkey and roast pork and all the usual Christmas fare was laid out on the dining room table and each one helped themselves with much laughter and happiness. Gail looked at the people around her and knew she would keep this picture in her heart forever. She quietly left the room and went to her suite. Her bags were ready packed except for one suitcase where she would pack her last bit of clothing in. She planned to leave the day after Christmas while the family was still in high spirits and not feel sad.

Later the children all came to her room and they all sat on the bed as they had done so many times before. Veronica had grown into a young lady and was leaving soon for a renowned finishing school for girls. Jackie was a tall gangly boy who would soon be a man. He would be at home for another year after which he was going to attend a college for boys. Little Michael had grown from a toddler to a boy who had discarded his insecurity to an outgoing child who laughed a lot. Gail hoped he would stay like that and not revert back to the way he was when she fist arrived.

'You must send me e-mails' Gail said to them 'and tell me how you are progressing.'

'We will Site' Jackie said.

'Veronica, make sure you take your laptop with you when you go. I want to know all about your new school.'

'Of course, Site, I will always keep in touch. You must also let us know how you are doing.'

'You can bet on that.' Gail said.

'Jackie you must teach Michael on the computer so he can also send me messages.'

'Yes, you must, please Jackie.' Michael said pleadingly.

When the children left Anton came to her room and sat at the desk.

'There are some things that I would like to say Gail.' She knew she also wanted to say some things to him and was happy to have this opportunity.

'I was sceptical about the idea of introducing a granny to my children but it was the best thing that could have happened. The children have benefited and so have I. and I hope that you did as well.'

Gail smiled. She knew she did not have to say anything after all as Anton had understood everything very clearly.

'I just wanted to make the final payment although it will in actual fact be impossible to pay for your service which was amazing and very unique.'

He handed Gail a cheque and she put it into her bag without looking at it.

She knew it would be generous and she stood up and hugged him.

'You have my e-mail details, please keep in contact.'

'I will and I expect to hear all the news of your new venture/'

When he left, Gail sat for a while just staring into space. She was determined to not let emotion take over. There was a new job waiting and she would survive.

The cab arrived early the next morning and it was only Ursula who saw her off with a hug. She put a small package into Gail's hand as she closed the car door. With a last wave the cab drove away. Gail did not look back but instead closed her eyes to keep her emotions in check.

*　　*　　*　　*

Gail's heart was pounding. She had taken a travelling tablet after breakfast and knew she would have to take another one once she had settled in her luggage. She was always on her nerves when she needed to travel and preferred to be at the airport early. Once she had her boarding pas safely in her bag and had gone through to international departures, she ordered a pot of tea and made herself comfortable for the wait before boarding. She opened her bag to pay for the tea, and her eyes fell on the cheque that Anton had given her. She took it out and looked briefly at the amount, not really registering what it was. Then putting it back in a more secure section in her bag, something triggered an alarm in her mind, and she took the cheque out again. Surely, the amount could not be right?

Carefully she took out her reading glasses and looked at the cheque again. Now her heart sent off little flutters in her chest as she took a few seconds to let the amount sink in. She knew Anton was a wealthy man, but his generosity stunned her. She put the cheque back in her bag and wondered if it could be deposited in another country?

Gail looked around her and saw a foreign exchange window not far away and went to enquire if she could do it. It turned out to be an agency for her own bank, and she made the deposit right away. Relieved, she found a comfortable chair and picked up a magazine from a table nearby.

Her concentration was however not on the magazine in her hand, instead the amount written on the deposit slip kept popping up and she found herself smiling at the people as they walked past.

The flight was full, but Gail felt calm. She also knew she would not have felt so if she had not taken the second tablet. Soon she would fall asleep and when she woke up, would be in another country.

Chapter Ten

AN ASIAN MAN, OF medium height with a slim body, dressed in a white shirt, black trousers and matching jacket complete with blue crest embroidered on the pocket, was flashing a board with her name on, which she noticed straight away, as she emerged from the glass sliding doors. She raised her hand and he moved forward to take her luggage.

He bowed to her before addressing her. 'Madam Gail?' She nodded and followed him to a car with a blue logo on the door that matched the logo on his jacket pocket. He opened the door for her and she climbed in. He first closed the door, and then put the luggage in the boot of the car, before getting in.

There were people, so many people, Gail thought, milling around and shouting from one side to another. It was all very exciting and she sat forward to watch the bustling crowds as they moved ahead at a slow pace.

The driver drove slowly until they left the city and then picked up speed.

She watched the landscape flitting by and the strangeness of it amazed her.

No conversation was passed between passenger and driver and she relaxed.

They must have covered at least fifty kilometres she calculated, before they stopped at tall wrought iron gates. The same logo was fixed on the gates, as was on the car. Gail saw now that it was a blue background with a snow capped mountain. The gates were opened by remote and they drove through. Without looking behind her Gail knew the gates would close.

She sat up very straight now to look at her surroundings of cultured lawns and flowerbeds, in colours so exotic, that it looked artificial. On the rise a building of great beauty awaited them. The curled up gables were almost black in colour with motives of bright orange, yellow and turquoise adorning them.

When the driver opened the door for Gail the sound of wind chimes came floating on the breeze. She looked around and saw what looked to her like hundreds of flutes dancing in the wind. She stood and took a deep breath savouring the sweet smell of lilies which grew nearby.

Oh! She thought, I hope that I will be happy in this beautiful place.

Intricate carved, wooden double doors stood open. Gail climbed the three stairs which were wide, and also made from wood, and were carved at the sides. A small woman stood waiting for her, and bowed low before waving her inside with a delicate hand. She was smiling and Gail bowed her head before entering. Little beads of sweat from nervousness felt cold on her forehead, and her heart was pounding in her chest. What if she had made a mistake, what if she did not fit in here? These thoughts flickered through her head as she followed the woman, who she saw had on soft slippers. She looked at her own travelling shoes, and knew she would have to get a new wardrobe for starters. She hoped that there was someone who spoke English, so that they could communicate, otherwise she would be totally lost.

They passed through a cool open area, with low couches surrounding a very low, wide coffee table. Carved screens were placed at two corners of the area, with a soft light behind the screens, creating a peaceful and calming atmosphere. Gail felt her body responding as her nervousness calmed down. The room she was shown to, was furnished with a cream coloured bed cover, and a light green throw draped at the bottom of the low bed.

The bed was no more than a few inches from the floor, and she knew she would have to get used to it. 'Phew' she thought, the list of getting used to, was growing longer and longer. The woman clapped her hands twice and a young girl appeared as if by magic. She bowed to Gail who did the same, and then spoke in clear English. Relief washed over Gail as a deep sigh escaped her.

'My name is Lani, we welcome you most honoured lady, to our humble home, and hope you will be very happy here with us.'

'Oh! I am very happy indeed to be here, thank you for having me in your beautiful home.'

'Please rest and refresh, we will meet with Mr Lai in the garden in an hour. Nahne will help you to unpack and to prepare a relaxing bath.'

Gail wanted to refuse, but thought she needed all the help she was offered, and bowed instead.

She stood at the low window, which was not made from glass, but a sheer rice paper. She could not see much through it, and decided that she would take a walk outside later, to settle her trembling heart.

Slowly she sat on the low bed and watched as Nahne packed her clothes in the low closet. The wood of the doors was very thin and delicately carved, and Gail saw as the doors were opened, that there were some kimonos hanging on one side. Beneath them, was an array of soft slippers placed neatly on a shelf.

When Nahne finished unpacking, she stored the cases on top of the cupboard and went into the adjoining bathroom where she opened the taps to let the water run into the bath. Gail caught the scent of lavender and when she entered the bathroom, a pleasant aroma enveloped her. In a small container on a low dresser she saw a scented candle. The water looked very inviting and then she heard the sliding door made from rice paper closing behind her. Absolute bliss, Gail thought as she climbed into the sunken bath, another first for her. The bath was flush with the floor and not very deep and somehow it did not phase her. Scented vapours enveloped her and she relaxed for a few moments before sponging herself with an outsize sponge. On the low stool nearby a big soft cream coloured towel was conveniently placed. Folded on the dresser was a light blue robe which Gail put on after drying herself.

The bath made her feel relaxed and she lay on the bed thinking she would just rest for a short while before dressing and instantly fell asleep.

When she awoke with a start she saw that a kimono was laid out on the chair with a pair of slippers to match. She knew everything would fit even before putting it on. The figure reflecting in the long mirror on the wall looked strange but pleasant and Gail smiled to her image. Look who I am the look said, look where I am. She brushed her hair back and put on a soft coloured lipstick and then Nahne was there to take her to the garden where Mr Lai was waiting with Lani the young girl she met earlier. Mr Lai stood up as did the young girl and they bowed to her and she did the same. Then he waved with his hand for her to sit down. He spoke in English with a marked accent 'We are very happy to have you with us.'

'I am happy to be here.' Gail said lowering her head and knew the ritual of welcoming was now complete.'

'Lali' he said' will show you around later but now we will first get to know each other.'

True to his word, many questions were asked both by him and then by her. Nahne brought small bowls with delicious sweetmeats and fruit cut into flowers and placed them on the small table in the centre. A clear liquid was poured into small cups. Gingerly Gail tasted the liquid and was pleasantly surprised at the refreshing mint taste causing a soft tingling sensation which seemed to dance on her tongue.

Lali went with Gail as they walked from room to room where the layout and furnishings were stark and beautiful. Every item enhanced the area in a way that gave off a feeling of serene calm and she wondered if she would get used to it. They went out to the garden again and saw Mr Lai had left. It was truly a beautiful place and Gail hoped she could be there for a while. No children were about and she was getting anxious and turned to the girl. 'Lali, where are the children?'

Lali smiled. 'They will soon be here. They went with their aunt to do some shopping.'

Their excited laughter announced them. A small woman, dressed in traditional kimono with a long ornamental pin in her hair, was with them. The woman was delicate and beautiful. Gail felt big and clumsy just looking at her. She bowed towards her and Gail did the same and one by one the four children who ranged from eleven down to four did the same holding their hands in the prayer position in front of them. Gail bowed in turn to each of them and then they all sat down.

"My name is Sa Ami, I am their aunt. My brother was looking forward to have you here with them.'

'Thank you' Gail said. 'I have already met with him.'

'The children will be tired now' Sa Ami made a drooping face 'we have done much shopping' and she winked at Gail. Gail liked her from the start and hoped they would get on well.

They sat for a while, Sa Ami, Lali and Gail, just chatting and asking questions before Sa Ami announced she had to leave. Gail said she should also rest for a short while and went to her room.

She saw another kimono laid out on her bed with matching slippers so she knew she had to dress for dinner. She had more than an hour to spare so she took out her laptop and sat on the top end of the bed and perched her laptop on her knees. Opening her e-mail file she saw messages from Veronica and Jackie with a message added from little Michael, and right at the end, one from Ursula. She smiled as she thought about the way her life had changed once more. A whole new world was enfolding with her at the centre of it all.

Her fingers moved easily on the keys as she gave them a detailed report of what she had experienced over the past few days and copied all her children in, even though there were no messages from any of them, and closed her laptop to begin preparing herself for dinner.

Lali came to fetch her and Gail admired her clothes. The kimono she had on was of a turquoise material inlaid with gold. Her long gold earrings nearly reached her shoulders and her eyebrows had a gold shimmer to them. As Gail followed Lali she could not help wondering what the official position was on this beautiful young girl.

Mr Lai and the children were seated on cushions around a low table.

She was shown to her place next to Mr Lai and Lali sat down next to her.

Gail watched with downcast eyes what they did and followed their actions.

Nahne served small bowls of different dishes. Gail waited to first see what Mia and Lali did before se attempted to take anything. Although everything looked strange to her, she also knew that she would have to eat something if she was to survive in her new surroundings. She took small amounts of two dishes near to her and when tasting it was pleasantly surprised at the delicate taste, so she tried two other dishes.

When the ritual of dinner was complete she had not eaten very much but preferred it that way. She first had to find out if the food agreed with her sensitive constitution. The children left with Nahne and the three of them sat quietly for a while before Mr Lai spoke.

'Lali is my younger sister. She will be here for the next two weeks but must then return to her work in the city. As I explained to you on the e-mail, my wife is in hospital. She is very ill and can have no visitors except myself and that is why the children need a grandmother.'

Gail once again did not know what her response should be so waited with downcast eyes. She had studied local customs on her flight from a book she bought at the airport and hoped she was getting it right.

'Lali will be with you for the next few days to explain more. Are your quarters comfortable?'

"Yes, thank you very much. What time shall I be expected to report in the morning?'

'Oh' Lali said. 'We will begin right away. We will go to the children now.'

Lali rose from the table and Gail followed her.

They went to the wing where the children had their rooms. Gail saw that it was adjacent to her quarters and only a short passage separated them. She was happy about this and wondered where Lali slept. She was taken there before going to the children. It was a bit further away and was furnished nearly exactly as the room Gail was in. The children had a section all to themselves. There was a large central room with cushions on the floor. A large plasma television screen was on a wall in the centre of the room and along one wall low cupboards formed a writing area with low stools for the children.

A large world map spanned one whole wall and there were two computer screens with more connections to black boxes that Gail had ever seen and she wondered what their functions were, but said nothing.

A low bookcase to the side with encyclopaedias filling the shelves was on one side of the room. It was obvious to Gail that learning and knowledge were very important here.

The children, all four of them, had their own rooms which were not very big and was sparsely furnished with a bed, flat on the floor, and a cupboard for clothes. In between two bedrooms was a bathroom that was shared and Gail was impressed with the way it was laid out. It was designed for company and togetherness yet each had their own space. The doors were sliding screens with rice paper in small frames making up the whole door. Lights above the beds were recessed but set in a way that sent its rays directly over the top end of the bed so that reading was not strained. All this she noticed with one sweeping glance. Lali took her to each child as they lay in their bed and formally introduced Gail whom she called Site as Gail had requested. Lali told them to look on her as their grandmother and Gail saw the dark eyes that turned to her gave no flicker of emotion and hoped that she could change that one day.

Tiredness was like a heavy blanket that enveloped Gail. Her body felt like brittle glass shards and she decided to have another bath to relax herself.

She lit the scented candle and filled the bath halfway with warm water.

Afterwards she rubbed her body with a herbal cream and sat for awhile on the low bed. Soon she would be asleep but at that moment a strong feeling of loneliness was making her feel emotional. She sat very still and slowly she felt it leave her. She was in a strange place, a strange country and she was a sixty-six year old granny among strangers. She climbed under the covers and said a simple prayer to keep her and her own family and the family she left in Austria as well as her new family safe. Sleep came quickly and when she awoke the sun was shining softly through her window covered in rice paper.

Nahne entered the room quietly with a tray with one single cup on and set it down on the floor next to the bed. She took out a kimono from the cupboard and laid it on the bed. A pair of matching slippers was placed on the floor. Gail drank the fragrant tea and then got out of bed. Her new life was about to begin and she was ready.

Nahne prepared breakfast for them in the kitchen. Small bowls of cereal with yoghurt and fresh fruit were on the table. The tea she poured into small cups was black and lightly sweetened and tasted different from the cup that was brought to her room, Gail found the tea refreshing and she tasted a hint of mint. The cereal she knew she would have to get used to although the fruit was delicious. Strawberries were cut into small wedges, with chopped apple and nuts, which she ate with a dressing of yoghurt. Everything had a delicate look about it and tasted very refreshing.

Mr Lai had already left for work and it was Gail and the children who sat around the low table. The children would be leaving for school in a short while and she planned to take a walk to familiarise herself with the surroundings. Mr Lai did tell her that her stay would be until his wife came home from hospital but did mention that his wife was expected to be there for some time. Gail had read about the protocol of the country while in the plane and so refrained from helping Nahne clear the table. There was nothing of the ease with which she helped Ursula, so she laid her serviette on her plate and left the room. When the children returned from school they would have their first private visit with her, so for the next few hours, she was free to do as she pleased. Outside the heat was like a solid wall and Gail put on the floppy hat that was left on her bed.

She walked slowly as she inspected the gardens and was delighted with the array of colours and fragrances bombarding her senses. Small birds flew in and out of nests which hung from the branches of a gnarled tree.

The birds seemed not to mind her presence at all while bees flitted from flower, to flower buzzing away happily creating background sounds for the display before her. She came to an intricately carved wooden bench standing in the shade under a tree and sat down. It was a pleasant setting and her thoughts soon drifted into space to her children in South Africa. What would they be doing, she wondered?

The feeling of pleasure that was derived from a family visit was totally lost for the younger people. This pastime will no doubt catch up with them later when they were older, and their eyes grew dim while the computer screen grew dimmer and more blurred by the day. She herself spent as little time as possible with her laptop and felt the strain very quickly.

Surprised at the figure walking toward her, Gail had to shake her head to clear the mist that had engulfed her brain.

'Nahne said I would find you here. Is everything all right?' Her voice was soft and pleasant when she spoke.

'Oh yes! Thank you Lali it is so pleasant out here and my thoughts just wandered out of control.'

Lali smiled and sat next to Gail. She put her head back and took a deep breath.

'I should spend more time outside. One forgets how pleasant it is.'

They sat for a short while in silence and then Lali said. 'Tell me about yourself. I am curious that you should take such an assignment. Where do you come from? Do you have a family?'

'Lali this could take a long time and later when we know each other a bit better I will tell you about my family. I come from South Africa. Do you know it at all?'

'No, not really, but I know where it is on the map.'

'Africa' Gail said 'is like a granny with a large lap, and on her lap, she holds the people of Africa. They are varied in colour and size. Black, white, yellow, brown, old and young, rich and poor, and they are all smiling most of the time.

'That sounds so interesting do you think I could visit you there when you return?'

'That will be lovely. I am not sure when I will be back there but I would be honoured if you came for a visit.' Gail put her hand on the girl's arm.

'I live near to the sea in the most beautiful part of the world that you could ever imagine.'

'Then it is done. We will keep in touch via e-mail and I will visit even if it is next year or later.'

'The people' Gail said 'are friendly and respectful and mostly happy. although there are many poor and homeless.'

'As there are here' Lali said 'but our people are less friendly and not sharing but very respectful of each other.'

'We will learn from each other.' Gail said and Lali nodded her head.

They got up from the bench and slowly walked back to the house as the heat outside had become unbearable.

At four in the afternoon the group was in the study. It was still hot outside but it was cooler inside the house.

Lali first spoke to the children in Japanese and then repeated it in English so Gail knew what was being said.

'Site will be with us while mammie is in hospital. I will have to leave soon to go back to work so Site will make sure you are all ok.'

'How long will Site be here?' Mia asked.

'We don't know yet, but it could be for three or four months.'

'What about our homework?' Nari asked.

'I have arranged with your teachers that all your work will be done after school so you do not have to be worried about doing it at home.'

'She can't even speak Japanese.' Fing piped up in English.

'Oh, we know that.' Lali said. 'But you will be able to practice your English.'

Gradually Gail felt as if she was accepted by the children in a guarded kind of way. She kept a low profile and felt comfortable just sitting in the lounge or outside where the children could see her. When she saw them looking at her she waved and smiled and after a few days it was the children who waved before she did.

On the Friday, Sa-Ami came to the house and told Gail she would fetch her and the children the next morning to take them shopping and later to lunch.

Gail was happy about that and looked forward to the next morning. She had not had the opportunity to go anywhere as yet and she knew the children also needed a few things for school.

They were all ready and waiting when Sa-Ami arrived in her car and Gail climbed in the back leaving the front seat for Nari. She had soon realised that women took a respectful stance where men were concerned and Nari took his position of eldest son very seriously.

Throngs of people were everywhere as the car inched forward until they found a parking space in a large car park.

It was a long walk to the shops further on in vast buildings with different cubicles of small shops advertising their wares. It was very crowded and Gail held Fing and Whan's hands not to loose them as they followed the others. The noise of chattering filled her ears and the smell of food cooking was everywhere.

Sa-Ami led them to an open area and asked to see their lists that they had prepared so she could take them to the right shops. They went from stall to stall until all the items on their respective lists were ticked off. Each carried their own parcels except for Fing who gave his parcel to Mia. They found an open table with long benches on the outskirt of the hall and placed their orders for refreshments with the young women who came to their table. Sa-Ami ordered for Gail wile the children each ordered what they wanted. The waitress wrote nothing down but returned a while later with their order exactly as it was ordered.

The children were chatting excitedly to each other while they ate their food and Sa-Ami leant closer to Gail.

'Are you coping with the family?'

'I think so' was Gail's reply 'it will take a bit of time to understand each others' needs better but we seem comfortable together.'

'I am glad to hear that, they have had a difficult time with their mother so ill and my brother has been under a great strain. Soon Lali will leave to go back to work and he will be depending on you.'

'I am happy that I can help.' Gail said while looking at the children to make sure they were still alright.

Sa-Ami saw Gail looking at the children and knew they were in good hands.

Gail looked at Sa-Ami again and said 'I need you to explain to me what my duties are. Nahne is very good in communicating and Mia will translate, but if I know beforehand then I can prepare more easily.'

Sa-Ami nodded and then went into detail as to how the arrangement should be. At the end Gail had a clearer picture in her mind and felt more at ease. She knew she would have to spend more time with the children individually to be of notable assistance and knew that, that was not a problem at all. Whan and Fing would be together most of the time and Mia and Nari usually did their homework together if they had anything to do. Her mind was already planning how she could allocate individual time to each one.

They finished their meal and walked back to where the car was. Gail saw Fing dragging behind and realised she must be tired so she gave her parcel to Mia to carry and picked Fing up. Gail was surprised to feel how light she was as she put her head down on Gail's chest. Before they reached the car she was fast asleep.

When they arrived home Gail carried Fing to her room where she covered her with a light blanket. Gail knew she would be asleep for a while giving her time to pack her own shopping away.

She found Mia and Nari in the lounge playing a board game and she sat watching them. When Whan came in to the room, he went straight to Gail and climbed on her lap. Gail gently drew him closer to her and he put his head on her chest. Nobody said anything but the cosy togetherness felt like the blanket she had covered Fing with. Gail knew the younger children missed their mother and she was happy that she could be with them. After all, she reasoned, that was what grannies were there for.

* * * *

All too soon Lali was ready to leave and Gail knew she would miss her. They liked each other from the start and exchanged e-mail addresses and promised to keep in touch.

That evening, after the children were tucked in bed, Gail took out her laptop and logged on to her e-mail.

There were messages from Ursula and the children and even from her own children. Well, she thought, let me tell them about my new family.

Gail told Ursula about her new family and when she was finished she copied her message to her own children. No harm in letting them know that she was a valuable asset and meant something to someone.

She told them about their visit to the market and about the children and Lali and Sa-Ami and Nahne but said nothing about Mr Lai as she knew he would not like to be discussed by strangers.

With Lali gone, Gail depended on Mia and Nari to translate when she wanted to talk to Nahne whose communication skills were very good but sometimes words had to be exchanged. The children took this in their stride which was a blessing. Gail noticed that there was not much interaction with Mr Lai and his children, nothing like Anton with his family. She felt sorry for the children who did not receive much love and tried to make her time with them more personal, especially for Whan and Fing who were still so young. Once a week Sa-Ami fetched them to get their supplies from the market and have lunch with her so she could catch up with the events that took place during the week. Gail knew that Sa-Ami spoke to Mr Lai, her brother, on a regular basis. Mr Lai was very often not at home and Gail knew he must be a very busy man and wondered about his wife, and the illness that she suffered from. Gail had asked Sa-Ami about this but did not get a satisfactory answer, so did not mention it again.

There was no other mode of travelling to be seen and Gail missed her scooter so when she saw a mother riding a bicycle with her small child in a basket mounted on the front of the cycle she gave it some thought. Her legs and particular her knees would not stand up to the strain but perhaps she should try. Not even as a young girl had she ridden a bicycle as she had found it difficult. She missed being able to explore the surroundings and made a mental note to mention this to Sa-Ami when she saw her again. Another solution was sure to be found, if she tried.

Usually after dinner she had all the children together for a short while so they could chat about their day and sometimes she told them stories. Little Fing loved the 'Three Bears' and this story was repeated many times. Gail also told them about the life in South Africa and they asked her many questions. To them it was like a fantasy which could not be real. Everything was so different, so bold they said and intense, and Gail even began to think like they did as the calm and gentle way of life around them grew on her.

The next time Sa-Ami came Gail asked her about a way that she and the children could explore the surrounding area.

'I am sorry' Sa-Ami said 'we should have arranged something sooner.

I will ask the driver to take you and the children out on Sundays. Will ten o'clock suit you?'

'That will be wonderful' Gail said 'how long will we have him for?'

'He will be available for as long as you like but I suggest you not stay out later than four so the children can prepare for school.'

Gail was very pleased with the offer and asked whether they could use him from the next day to which Sa-Ami assured them he would be ready.

'I will supply him with a list of interesting places and you can arrange with him where to go. Nahne will prepare a picnic basket in case you get hungry.'

When the driver arrived on the Sunday morning they were all ready and Nahne carried the basket to the car.

Gail got into the back with Mia, Whan and Fing and Nari sat upfront with the driver. He was quite the person in charge when they went anywhere and Gail knew it was his honoured place.

Surprisingly the driver spoke English well and showed them the list Sa-Ami had given to him.

They discussed the places and time allocations and Gail left it for Mia and Nari to decide where they should go to for their first visit.

The driver skirted the busy town area and soon they were on a country road. It was not long before another town came into sight and Gail sat forward to take it all in.

Although the town was only two hours away there was a marked difference in the low buildings and the gardens. Fing climbed on Gail's lap to see more and Whan craned his neck to look out of the window. The people they saw wore more coloured clothing and there was an air of festivity around them.

'Festival day, today' the driver said. 'We stop for refreshment soon.'

Gail hoped they would stop in town but the driver carried on till they had left the town and then turned off on to a sand road. On the edge of a dam he stopped and took two blankets from the back of the car and spread them out on the grass. The driver fetched the baskets and Gail helped him to unpack the food.

The scene before them was beautiful. The water shone like golden sparklers and in the distance a mountain looked blue and hazy. Everything looked calm and serene and after they finished eating and the baskets were once again the car Gail took a short walk with the children to explore their surroundings. The children were excited and ran all over the place so Gail was content to go back to the blanket and sit down where she could see them. The air was pure and crisp with a hint of fragrance from a nearby bush with delicate pink flowers. She felt her eyes become heavy so she got up again and slowly walked to where the children were playing a game. She smiled as she watched their enjoyment and memories of the times when she and her late husband took their own children out to a picnic came flooding in.

It was something about the open air that triggered a sense exuberance to fill one's very being.

They stayed there for a while and when she saw their energy fading she called them back.

Saturdays were always a flurry of getting ready and preparing the lists for the market and their morning with Sa-Ami and was their highlight of the week. That was before they began going out on Sundays. By Thursday the children had already decided which way they were going and by Friday Nahne had her list for supplies ready. Gail often wondered why Nahne was always on duty but knew it was not her place to question this arrangement. Surely she should have some time off to visit her own family? Did she even have any family? Gail wondered about these things and it was while they were all enjoying a picnic high on a mountain pass that Gail asked Mia about this.

'Nahne has no family. We are the only family she knows. She was working with Fathers' parents and when he married mom she was part of the dowry.'

'Do you think she would come with us next Sunday?' Gail asked.

Mia thought about this and then spoke to Nari in Japanese. Gail could see that he was not in agreement and then he addressed himself to Gail.

'We will first ask her if she wants to come and then we will speak to my father.

'That will be nice.' Gail replied and left the matter there.'

They were usually all tired on Sunday evenings and retired early to be refreshed for school. A list was pinned to the green felt board in the study room showing the places they wanted to visit while the places they had been to were marked with a red dot. This list grew as the children thought of other places and from suggestions that Sa-Ami made. Gail was the willing participant and at night when she checked her e-mails she explained in detail to her own family where they had been. She wondered if they sometimes thought she was making up these escapades and decided to start taking pictures with her digital camera to include with her messages.

Gail noticed a change in the manner of messages from her children as if they admired her for her achievements, but felt she was overdoing things. She ignored their remarks of concern or when they asked what her plans were for returning home, and instead told them about the visits they were planning for their next outing. In any case, she thought, what would she do at home? Die of boredom and neglect? No she had other plans before she succumbed to that.

The next Sunday there was even more excitement as Nahne, decked out in a new kimono and a new pair of sandals waited with them. The picnic basket stood ready with special treats to mark the occasion. Gail was formerly informed by Mr Lai that if they did not mind it would be an honour for Nahne if she could accompany them. Nahne, although she showed a calm exterior, was obviously nervous and excited. She sat with Gail in the back of the car where Fing climbed on Gail's lap and folded her hands as if it was what she normally did.

For this special day a visit to a shrine was first on the list and then a nearby shopping mall which was nothing like the market they went to on Saturdays with Sa-Ami. Afterwards they would stop for a picnic in a pleasant spot.

Nahne fitted in with ease and exchanged pleasantries with the driver.

With the help of Mia or sometimes even Nari, Gail could hold a conversation with Nahne and the morning passed most pleasantly.

An agreement was also made that Nahne would join them every second Sunday for their exploratory visits.

Amazingly Gail picked up words here and there and found she could more or less understand what was being said. The driver had become quite friendly on their outings and sometimes romped around with the children when they played. It was also noticeable that a friendship of sorts was developing between Nahne and the driver and Gail watched this quietly saying nothing to upset the harmony. Life is good and she was more than content. She knew it would end one day but for now she was happy.

On a Monday morning after a pleasant outing on the day before Gail saw a new entry had been added to the list on the wall in the study area. It was written in a different handwriting and Gail knew instinctively that it was written by Mr Lai. She never got to know his first name and knew she never would but that was fine with her. 'Visit to hospital' it said so Gail telephoned Sa-Ami and told her about the entry on the list and Sa-Ami said she would get back to Gail.

Four months had passed since Gail's arrival and she wondered what it could mean but she did not dwell on the possibilities.

Mr Lai called them into the lounge to tell them that they would be visiting their mother at the hospital on Sunday. He would take them and the driver would fetch them from there so that he could stay a bit longer with his wife.

The children's mood changed after that moment to a more serious and withdrawn demeanour. Gail was to accompany them so that she could manage the children so his wife would not be stressed. Well, Gail thought to herself that is exactly what grannies are there for, and it made her happy to be of some assistance. She was after all a granny and she loved being just that.

Sa-Ami brought a small gift when she fetched them on the Saturday and asked Mia to give it to her mom the next day, explaining that it contained the sweets her mother liked. Mia took the gift to her room to keep till the next day.

Gail took special care to get the children ready for their visit to the hospital and Nahne checked them at the door to make sure there was nothing out of order. Mia held the gift that Sa-Ami brought tightly in her hand.

Mr Lai was waiting in his luxurious car and Nari got into the front with him.

The journey took almost an hour and was made mostly in silence. The children were subdued and Mr Lai looked as if he was concentrating on the road which was just as well as they would not know what to talk to him about anyway. There was not any tangible emotion between father and children and Gail wondered how it would be with their mother.

Mr Lai walked in front with Nari behind him and then Mia. Gail held hands with Whan and Fing who walked with her. She felt their uncertainty like a current emitting through their small hands. She longed to hug them but knew she should not.

The hospital was pleasant and sunlight streamed into rooms through large glass arched panels in the roof. Furnishings in the lounge area consisted of low couches upholstered in soft green and blue and were arranged in groups around low carved coffee tables. Here and there people were sitting in groups and some people wore soft blue loose kimonos that were tied at the waist. Gail knew that they must be the patients.

Mr Lai led them to a room at the far side of a passage and entered through soft blue coloured double doors. Inside the room was of medium size and pleasantly furnished. There was only one bed and the woman looked small sitting up against large pillows.

Gail handed the children to Mia and went back to the lounge area to wait for them.

Watching the people around her, she picked up when they were happy or when they were sad. She was so engrossed in her observations that she did not even notice the children walking towards her.

'The driver will meet us outside.' Nari said.

'Oh! You startled me. My thoughts were really far away.'

Nari smiled and took her hand to help her up. This action surprised Gail as he was not one to show concern.

'Thank you Nari, you are very kind.'

Outside the driver was waiting and opened the door of the car when he saw them approaching. Gail was acutely aware that the children were emotional and said nothing. They drove a short way and then the driver pulled up at a roadside tea garden. There were tables and chairs in the shade of a big tree and they all sat there and a waiter served them almost immediately. It was only when their order arrived that the children started talking.

When they spoke it was not about their mother but about their surroundings and Gail chatted along with them.

A half hour later they were on their way home again. Fing fell asleep with her head on Gail's lap and Whan soon closed his eyes as well next to Mia who sat in the corner lost in her own thoughts. Nari was chatting to the driver and Gail realised that in all the time they spent together she had never learned what his name was, and made a mental note to rectify this oversight.

Nahne was waiting for them at the door when they stopped and Gail knew she was most probably watching at a window for their arrival.

Although emotion was not usually evident she knew that it was there but not openly displayed. Nahne must also be anxious for news from Mrs Lai and Gail knew she herself had nothing to tell her. She hoped that Mia would be more helpful.

Gail waited until she saw them all go inside before she spoke to the driver not knowing whether her actions would be frowned on.

'Excuse me for asking but I realised today that I do not know your name and respectfully ask that you should tell me what it is.'

The driver took his cap off and bowed down to her.

'I am Mr Ming and am honoured to be the driver for Mr Lai for many years.'

'Thank you Mr Ming for looking after us so well.' Gail bowed and walked away.

That evening Mr Lai once again called her into the lounge.

'Mrs Lai will be staying in hospital for a while longer so I will be honoured if you could stay.'

'How is Mrs Lai?' Gail asked.

Mr Lai dropped his eyes to the floor and then back to Gail and his expression showed pain.

'More tests will have to be made and all will depend on what the outcome is.'

'I will stay of course, for as long as you need me.'

'Thank you' he said bowing his head 'I will of course make compensation.'

Gail knew it was a statement not to be contested and bowed her head and waited for him to leave the room first before going to her own quarters. She also knew that he would be spending time with each child that evening to re-assure them and that she would wait before going to check on them. She took out her laptop and checked her messages and saw there was one from Jake. It was really only a greeting but it made her happy so she replied telling him about their visit to the hospital and that she would be staying a while longer and that she was well, then logged off. The day had been one filled with emotion and she felt drained. When she thought Mr Lai had completed his rounds she started with Nari because she knew Mr Lai would have been there first.

Nari was in bed with a book open next to him. She bowed before sitting on the bed.

'Was your mom happy to see you Nari?'

She thought she would ease him in slowly before asking more important questions.

'Yes, and I was happy also.'

'She must be very proud of you.'

He nodded but said nothing so she continued.

'I had an e-mail message from my son Jake today. He sends his best wishes to you all.'

'Thank you Site, please tell him I am happy to accept his good wishes and also send my own to him.'

'I will certainly do that but I would like to let him know how you are.'

She waited a while before he spoke again.

'You may tell him that my family and I will say special prayers for my mom so that she will be better soon.'

Gail got up and bowed before leaving him. She had managed to let him know that she as well as her family cared about them.

School holidays were commencing soon and Mr Lai informed them after dinner one evening that he had arranged for them to go on a trip. The children were excited and wanted to know more and for once he indulged them.

'It will be by boat. The journey will take three days to take you to a resort where you can enjoy yourselves for ten days before returning. Sa-Ami will take you shopping for new clothes before you go.'

Great excitement reigned that evening as the children told Gail about the place they were going to.

There, they told her, were many things to amuse them and after chatting to them she even became excited. Not only for the resort and its many attractions it offered, but for the boat ride as well. She had only once before been on a boat and was seasick the whole time spending every hour of the trip on her bunk. She felt then that she was in a nightmare and it was listed as one of her ten worst experiences. If only she had been warned she could have prepared herself with travel medication which she now knew she would have to do if she wanted to enjoy the trip. She made a mental note to stock up with enough medication for herself and the children.

Chapter Eleven

SA-AMI HAD A LONG list when she collected them and to Gail's surprise there were items marked for her as well. Three new garments made from soft fabric were included which Sa-Ami said would be for swimming.

The garments were to be worn over a full piece bathing costume and new colourful sandals were bought to match.

The children each had a variety of items as well as soft linen hats for the heat. Gail also got a hat and a large colourful bag for the beach. She wondered about the beach and asked Sa-Ami when they rested at their usual tea house.

'It is a beach but man-made.' She said. 'You will feel as if you are at the beach and you will enjoy it very much. You must take a book to read.'

Each day the excitement grew not only from the children but Gail as well and when the luggage was finally in the car they waved back at Nahne who waved to them from the doorway where she was standing. Gail knew she would miss Nahne and wished she was going with them but she knew she would be looking after Mr Lai while they were gone.

Dutifully the children had all taken their tablets from the day before as Gail did and she was looking forward to an enjoyable trip.

The boat was very large and the Japanese writing on the hull was translated by Nari as 'Mystical Queen.' Gail loved the name and held Whan and Fing by the hand as they walked up the steel stairs to the deck.

Polished brass was Gail's first impression. It was everywhere and gleamed like gold in the sun. Crew members dressed in white greeted all the passengers and checked their boarding passes to direct them to their quarters.

They had a suite on the top deck which was furnished in beautiful wood carved furniture. A basket of fresh fruit and nuts was on a round carved table on one side of the lounge. Three bedrooms led from the lounge area. Two of the bedrooms had single beds side by side and the third bedroom had a double bed and each bedroom had its own bathroom.

Their luggage was already there and a chambermaid was busy unpacking their smaller suitcases. The bigger ones would be left unopened until they got to the resort. Gail knew they were probably in one of the best suites and was happy about them all being together. She thanked Mr Lai in her heart and then wondered if it had perhaps been Sa-Ami. Well, whoever it was made her very happy.

When the maid left she gathered the children in the lounge. She knew it was not necessary to remind them to be careful but she said it anyway.

'Whan and Fing, you will be with me at all times. I want to see you every minute. Nari and Mia, check with me and let me know where you are at all times. Be careful do not go near any railings, and if the weather gets bad go to the cabin immediately.'

They both agreed and turned to leave but Gail called them back. 'Nari stay with Mia, and Mia make sure you are always with Nari. They nodded and left. Gail knew she had to let them go but worried anyway.

The enormity of her responsibility suddenly felt like a heavy load and although she knew the children were well behaved and usually careful she had to deliver her charges safe and sound when they returned home.

An hour later they all met for lunch in the vast dining room. Their table was near to the captains' table and she realised it went with the suite they were in. The food was excellent and afterwards she gave them all a tablet again which they dutifully swallowed to ward off any nausea.

There was an area demarcated for young children where they could play games and Gail left Whan and Fing there while she sat on the deck at mid-section with her book. She could see Mia and Nari further away and did not even realise that her eyes closed as sleep overcame her.

Later she collected Whan and Fing and took them back to their suite where they both fell asleep. Gail knew that the tablets had made them drowsy and together with the excitement and the car journey they would sleep for a while. She covered them with blankets and took a book and lay on her bed to rest while they were asleep. Soon her eyelids drooped and she drifted away.

More than an hour later she woke up and went to check on the children.

She smiled when she saw that Mia and Nari were also sound asleep on their beds. Gail fetched her book from her room and made herself comfortable in the small lounge.

It was close to five when the children woke up one by one.

'Did you have a nice rest Nari?'

'Gee, Site, I could hardly keep my eyes open but now I feel refreshed.'

'You have time for a bath before we go to dinner. Don't take too long though.'

Nari grinned at her and disappeared into the bathroom.

'Mia you can help me with Whan and Fing so long. We have a long evening ahead of us.'

Dinner was a grand affair. The captain stopped at all the tables and welcomed his guests. When he came to their table he first spoke Japanese and when Nari answered him he went over to English.

'We are honoured to have you all with us.'

Then he turned back to Nari.

'How is your mother?'

Nari answered in English. 'She is slowly getting better. Site is taking care of us until she returns home.'

The captain bowed to Gail and she knew she was honoured by his gesture and she dropped her head in acknowledgement. Once her position was established she knew she received the same attention as a parent would.

From then on Gail was greeted with respectful bows from any crew member that passed her, which she in turn would acknowledge by dropping her gaze.

The live show that evening was amazing. A conjurer performed impossible tricks that had the audience gasping. The children were enthralled and joined in with enthusiasm.

When they got back to the cabin Gail ordered a hot drink for all and once again gave them each a small white tablet. She knew this was necessary if they wanted to enjoy their stay on the ship.

The next morning an invitation was delivered to their suite. There was a sharp rap on the door and when Gail opened it a junior officer dressed in white presented a silver plate with a white envelope resting on it.

'What is this?' Gail asked her heart fluttering in her chest as her thoughts groped around in her head thinking it may be a message from Mr. Lai.

'With respect an invitation from the captain, requesting your presence, at his table for dinner this evening.'

Gail took the envelope and opened it. The card was printed in black ink and gold filigree was embossed along the edges.

'I will be honoured if you and all the children will join me at my table for dinner this evening.'

Gail bowed deep to the officer. 'Thank you. We are most honoured. What time will the captain expect us?'

'At 18h45 an officer will call for you, and chaperone you to the dining room.'

The officer bowed and so did Gail before closing the door.

'Nari, Mia' she called 'come and see what we have received.'

Nari was clearly in charge as he walked behind the officer who came to fetch them, with Mia behind him, and Gail holding hands with Whan and Fing bringing up the rear.

When they arrived at the table, the captain was already there and he stood up and bowed to them. They all bowed to him and then he waited till they were settled before sitting down.

Nari was seated next to the captain and then Mia, Whan, Gail and Fing. The table was attended to with great honour and the captain spoke alternately in Japanese and English. The food was excellent and presented in beautiful bowls resting on silver platters. Nari was clearly enjoying himself as he listened to the captain speaking while keeping his head at a slight angle in respect. Gail knew the younger children would be restless soon and wondered how long they had to stay at the table before they could get up. After the dessert was served she asked if she could be excused with the younger children, which she told them did not include Nari, who made his own decisions. She saw Nari bow his head to her and knew she had said the right things. The captain stood up again and waited till they left the table before he sat down with Nari still next to him. Gail felt very proud of Nari and she would report this to Sa-Ami when she saw her again.

In their suite Gail helped with bathing the little ones while Mia used the other bathroom. Once the children were in their night clothes they all sat in the lounge. Gail had ordered a hot drink for them from the kitchen and when it came she gave them each another tablet to keep them going. They chatted for a while and then the children retired to bed. Once they were settled Gail relaxed in a pleasantly warm bath after taking her own tablet. What a difference she thought, by taking a small white travel tablet, she could actually enjoy the cruise. Just goes to show with the right preparation one need not be stressed at all.

The next day was their last day on the boat as they planned to reach their destination during the night and passengers would embark after breakfast. Their return journey from the resort was going to be by plane and although Gail had in fact enjoyed the cruise, she was happy knowing the return journey, would not take as long.

Chapter Twelve

A BUS TOOK THEM TO their hotel and it was only when the luggage was packed on the awaiting trolley held firmly by a porter that they heard the noise coming from the beach.

Laughing and shouting intermingled with children crying and the thunderous crashing of waves filled the air and Gail stood transfixed at the scene which although a short distance away seemed to dominate everything.

People were everywhere and Gail tightened her grip on the two small hands she was holding. Whan and Fing pressed their bodies closer to Gail and she smiled thinking they were probably just as nervous.

Nari led the way with the porter wheeling their luggage behind him and then Mia followed with Gail still holding the hands of the little ones.

Inside the hotel foyer it was cool and pleasant as they waited for Nari to complete the paperwork. When Nari was finished he asked Gail to sign next to his signature, and after a copy was taken of her passport, they were taken to their suite.

As on the boat the suite was luxurious. There were three bedrooms each with their own bathroom on suite as well as a lounge area with a giant size television screen fixed to the wall and gave one the impression that they were in a private theatre.

Exhausted Gail sat down on a sofa to give her heart time to settle down while the children explored their rooms. All the travelling and excitement was taking its toll and she realised that she would have to take things slower for the next few hours.

'Mia, you and Nari take Whan and Fing to explore. You will hold their hands and not let them go. I need to take a little rest.'

Mia came to her and looked concerned. 'Are you alright Site? Do you need anything?'

'Some cold water will be nice.' Gail said with a smile.

Mia opened a cupboard and found a small fridge which she opened and took a bottle of chilled water out. She put the water and a glass on the small table next to Gail and waved as they left the room.

The bottle was cold to her touch and Gail held it to her cheek to cool herself down before taking a sip. She removed her sandals and put her feet up on the sofa and rested her head on a soft cushion. Her eyes closed almost immediately as sleep overtook her.

Upon waking it took Gail few minutes to clear her mind and to familiarise her surroundings. Slowly she got up and put on her sandals and then only did he inspect their suite. Her room had a double bed and a low dressing table, with a mirror that stretched nearly to the ceiling, Double sliding doors led to a wide balcony which overlooked a garden that was well kept with a manicured lawn area. Chairs and a small round table as well as two sun loungers were set out in a comfortable manner and bright orange cushions gave it a feeling of warmth. Gail immediately fell in love and knew she would enjoy sitting on the balcony sipping tea and eating small cakes. She sat for a while allowing the sun to caress her body and when the heat became too much she went inside to complete her inspection.

The children's rooms each had two single beds that were low on the ground and a low cupboard with drawers separated the beds. A tall reading lamp, with a cream velum shade made the whole room look elegant. Both rooms were the same and Gail saw that their clothes had already been unpacked. Amazed she realised that room service must have been in while she was sleeping.

After a refreshing shower she dressed in a fresh kimono and heard the children retuning. They were hungry and excited and quickly got ready for dinner.

The dining area was really large and the food was good although they did not linger as the children wanted to show Gail all the games and special attractions which catered for all ages ranging from toddlers to teens, and even adults. The variety and imagination that was used to create the area left Gail in awe.

Never before had she seen the likes of the presentation before her or the crowds that thronged the promenade. Lights lit up the swimming area where waves constantly crashed on the manmade beach and she saw people were swimming even at that late hour.

Noting that Whan and Fing were dragging their feet she took them back to their suite. Many days of entertainment awaited them but now they had to rest.

Days of enjoyment followed as Gail took her book each morning and positioned herself in a comfortable lounger in a shady spot where she could see the children. Although there was always a big crowd in the swimming area Gail had no problem keeping an eye on the children in her care. This was amazing she thought to herself on the first day when they swam. She was actually nervous when she saw all the people imagining that they all looked the same and then just like that she knew that the perception was in fact wrong because each one had their own image that differed completely from the other. This realisation made her smile and even when the man next to her looked at her peculiarly she felt like laughing out loud but somehow restrained herself.

Later in the afternoon they would all rest in their suite and then go the games area where they played the most amazing games. Gail sometimes joined in the fun and from there they went to dinner in the huge dining hall. After dinner they took a slow walk in the gardens and then went to their suite to bath. Dressed in their pyjamas they gathered around the big television screen for a while before going to bed.

This was a time when they were all relaxed, and the children although speaking English to Gail, would chatter to each other in their own language. Gail took more notice when they spoke to each other and now and then Nari or Mia would explain to her what was being said.

Before bedtime they each had a turn to tell the others about their day and once they were in bed Gail sat for a short while with each child just talking about whatever they felt like, before she turned in.

It was on a morning much like any other. Gail was on her usual lounger when an elderly man came to sit near her. She did not take any notice of the man until he spoke to her in English.

'Good morning madam, I hope you don't mind if I sit here and chat to you.'

Surprised Gail looked at the man who she saw was about her own age and although he looked Asian there was also a European look about him.

She raised her eyebrows but said nothing. It was unheard of for a man to address a woman without first being introduced. He immediately bowed his head while still seated and she did the same.

'My name is Mr Saan.'

'I will be most honoured if I may sit here and talk to you for a while.'

Gail dropped her book to her lap and waited for him to continue not saying a word.

'I have seen you with the children and am puzzled. You are obviously not Asian but they are.'

'I am their surrogate grandmother' she said 'their mother is ill in hospital so I am taking care of them until she is well again.'

He smiled at her. 'I am here with my grandchildren. That little girl there' pointing to a girl splashing about in the pool 'and my grandson' now pointing to a boy playing near the girl 'they are twins and are six years old.' Gail saw that the boy was a bit taller than his sister but their features were identical.

'Where are their parents?' She asked.

'Oh, they are on a second honeymoon.'

He smiled at her and looked toward his grandchildren. 'I offered to take care of them while they are away.' He paused for a while before continuing. 'My son works very long hours and they don't get much time to spend together.' He paused again. 'And my daughter-in-law was ill after she had a miscarriage not long ago.'

'Oh, I am sorry to hear that.' Gail said. 'It is important for a couple to have some quality time together. A mother is very much needed in a family and should be well taken care of.'

He bowed his head again. 'It is most kind of you to listen to me. We will meet again I hope.' He stood up, bowed and left.

What a nice man she thought picking up her book again.

At dinner time Mr Saan bowed to them as he passed by with his two grandchildren to a table further away. Once they had all been seated and ordered their meal he got up and told the children he would be back shortly. He walked back to the table where Gail and the children were and once again bowed towards them.

'Are you attending the magician show this evening?'

Every second night a magician show was held in the vast hall and Gail and the children had been there and enjoyed the performance immensely. The tricks of magic or whatever one should call it, was so expertly and convincingly performed, that they were all enthralled by it.

'Yes' Gail said 'we will see you there if you are also going, we are looking forward to the show.'

He bowed again and Gail dropped her head and he left.

When they entered the hall he came to them and after the customary bow which was given and returned, guided them to a table he had been sitting at. His two grandchildren were there and the children all started chatting away to each other.

The show was good as it usually was and afterwards Mr Saan invited them to the patio outside for a soft drink. The whole area was lit up with lights that shimmered like silver crystals with coloured lamps lower down towards the garden, and it had a mystical atmosphere. People sat everywhere on tables and on the grass as it was a warm evening. Mia took Whan and Fing by their hands and the children all started playing together. Somehow the holiday had taken on a different feeling and Gail knew the children were also happy. She sat on her lounger watching them and Mr Saan sat next to her keeping an eye on his grandchildren. It was an unspoken issue between them but they both knew what their responsibilities were.

'So tell me' Mr Saan said to Gail 'how is it that a woman of your culture has the position of grandmother to these children?'

Gail did not feel it appropriate to explain and said 'I was invited by a good friend and was honoured to help while their mother is ill. As their grandmother I have more respect and the children love me and I love them. They are my own and I care for them as such.'

Mr Saan bowed his head to Gail and she did the same.

'It is an honourable position. I am also honoured to have such good children.'

They sat quietly for a while and then he began telling her about his life.

'My son is in the diplomatic service and so he and his wife travel a lot.

They do take the children with sometimes and other times they stay with me. I have a suite in their home which is large, as they entertain guests on a regular basis. It is convenient for me to be near the children and for them to be near their children. In such a way we are all happy and feel secure within our family. My wife left this earth six years ago and I would have been lonely on my own.'

Gail knew how he felt after all she was also alone since the passing of her own husband. In truth it was that very loneliness that made her seek the closeness of a family. She also realised that she had not felt that way for a long time. The stay with Anton and his family, and now with Mr Lai, gave her a feeling of worth and comfort instead of the empty spaces that engulfed her while on her own. She smiled at Mr Saan and bowed her head.

*   *   *   *

Days were filled with sunshine and the children played with their new friends while Gail and Mr Saan sat in their loungers keeping an eye on them.

Evenings found them all together watching the live shows that made them laugh and they were all content. It was with sadness that Gail realised one morning that their time in this lovely place was nearing its end. She saw the children also felt the same and tried to cheer them up.

At the pool in his usual place on the lounger Mr Saan also felt it and he knew he would miss Gail and her companionship.

They had grown used to each other by just being there. When Gail arrived he stood up and bowed as she did.

When Gail was seated she took a note from her bag and handed it over to him. 'This is my e-mail address and contact numbers just in case you would like to contact me and tell me how you are doing.'

Mr Saan took the note and then from his pocket took out a card and handed it to Gail as he smiled. Their minds had thought along the same lines and she smiled while keeping her eyes lowered.

*　　*　　*　　*

The plane waiting for them on the runway was not very big and once inside Gail realised that it was probably a charter flight. The interior was luxurious and seats were spaced out allowing for comfort. Earlier Gail had dutifully given the children their tablet for travelling and then taken her own so that they could enjoy a stress free journey.

Three days it had taken them to reach their destination where they had a glorious holiday and now it would be less than two hours to fly home. What a wonderful world this was she told the children where they all sat strapped in their seats and they all agreed with her.

*　　*　　*　　*

Nahne was waiting at the door for them and when the car stopped she rushed down to help them get out. She took their hands and touched it to her cheek. Emotion was like a wave that washed over Gail as she felt the touch of Nahne's hand on her cheek. The children were in a circle around Nahne and she put her hands on their shoulders and guided them in. They were home again and yes! Life was good.

Although they were gone for nearly three weeks there were not many messages on Gail's laptop which was left at home and she relished the thought of telling everyone about their trip. First it was to Anton and his family then her own children where she went into more details. When she was finished she clicked on the 'send and receive' button and another message popped up. Mr Saan was home as well and wasted no time in making contact. Gail was happy and said so in her return message.

Mr Lai did not join them for dinner as he stayed over in the city so it was two days after their arrival that they first saw him. He was happy to see them and in a rare show of affection lifted Fing up on his lap and hugged Whan to his knees. He spoke softly to them in Japanese and they smiled. Gail was filled with emotion as she watched the father and children together in such a special way.

After dinner that evening they all gathered in the lounge and once Nahne took the children to bed Mr Lai asked Gail to stay.

He bowed his head and then told her how happy he was to have them back home again and how grateful he was that she took such good care of the children. He was very happy, he said, that Mrs Lai would finally be able to come home and be with her family. Gail bowed when she left the lounge but knew that there were issues that were not spoken of and knew that she would have to post an advertisement again. Her steps were slow as she made her way to her room.

Chapter Thirteen

GAIL HAD KNOWN THAT this day would come but still it was a jolt. Although she showed no emotion her heart was sad not only for herself, but for the children as well. They had grown fond of her and she had felt them creep into her own heart. Mr Lai, she could see, was also trying to control his own emotions especially when he was with the children. Nahne smiled but Gail saw her wipe a tear away when she thought nobody could see. She herself was sad but appeared cheerful for the children and told them how excited their mother was going to be to see them. She knew this was the truth, and her own spirits lifted thinking of Mrs Lai coming home.

An envelope with her cheque and a reference was given to Gail by Mr Lai as well as the contact number for a travel agency where he explained she could arrange for a ticket to any destination of her choice.

Gail took the envelope to her room and sat on the chair at the window for a while holding the envelope in her lap before opening it. It was after all a final task and she wanted to savour the few moments of her life as it had been. Slowly a feeling of excitement made her realise that this was not an ending but the beginning of a whole new adventure and she smiled as she opened the envelope.

The amount on the cheque was very generous and she held the paper to her heart.

For a weak moment she felt there was not enough money to ease her pain of leaving the children and then she realised that she had in fact become too attached to them, and that was a mistake. They were after all not her own children, and it was time to let them go. She made up her mind there and then that if she ever got an opportunity again for a similar assignment, she would not become so attached.

With a firm step she walked to the cupboard to take out her laptop. She opened it and re-read the past few e-mails.

*   *   *   *

Although Gail knew that she would have to choose a destination as a matter of urgency to allow enough time for any documents or visas to be issued she also knew that it was something she should think of very carefully. First of all she wanted to take a two week holiday to explore Japan as she had grown fond of the country and would in all probability never be there again. She telephoned Sa Ami who she knew was told of the arrangements by Mr Lai.

'I am sorry that you will be leaving us Gail but I am happy to know that the children's mother will be home soon. I think you are very wise and of course you must spend a few days in Tokyo it is a very interesting city.'

"Perhaps you can give me a few ideas how I can best use my limited time there?' Gail said.

'I will do better than that' Sa Ami said 'I am going to give your telephone number to a friend of mine who will be your guide.'

'Thank you Sa Ami that will be nice.'

After the telephone call Gail went to the kitchen where Nahne was busy preparing lunch for the children for when they got home from school.

Nahne smiled at Gail when she saw her and Gail was once again amazed at the transformation that Nahne had gone through since her arrival.

How wrong of her to have thought Nahne unemotional, when now she could clearly see a multitude of feelings, in the person before her. She realised that it was only be getting to know someone that one could recognise their feelings. In that moment Gail knew that it was not only Nahne that had been transformed, but herself as well.

The two of them sat together at the kitchen table chatting away until the children arrived. Gail looked at their excited faces with all the news of the day bursting to erupt and she knew that she would miss their togetherness more than she ever thought was possible.

When lunch was over Gail invited the children to sit with her in the garden for a while to share all their news. Mr Lai had informed the children earlier of their mothers' return and they looked forward to having her home but at the same time they were sad to know that Gail was leaving them.

'Will you come and visit us Site?' Mia asked.

'Mia I think it would be a good idea if you came to visit me at some time in the future. That way I can show you the beautiful country where I come from.'

Mia got up and hugged Gail 'Oh yes Site! I will do that as soon as I can travel alone.'

'Well', Gail said 'you can always come with Nari or even Sa Ami.'

Mia sat down again and Gail could see she was already making plans in her head and she smiled at Mia with affection.

The kimono that she chose was from soft silk in an almost eggshell colour and it felt cool on her body. A bright yellow comb was pinned in her hair and her sandals matched her ensemble. When Gail checked her appearance in the mirror she wondered if she would be able to take some things with her when she left. She had grown used to the clothing and felt comfortable wearing it.

Gail went outside and sat under the trees in the shade where it was cool and Nahne brought a tray with two small cups and a plate with delicate sandwiches. They poured the tea from the teapot and sat for a while enjoying the moment. Gail knew that Nahne had taken care of the children in their basic needs but it was Gail who had filled the void of their mothers' absence.

The bus dropped the children in the road close to the house and when the children saw Gail sitting in the garden they went to her. The younger two Whan and Fing hugged her and Mia sat down on the grass next to Gail. Nari preferred to stand.

'When are you leaving Site?' Mia asked in a serious voice.

Gail smiled 'Very soon.' She hesitated 'probably on Friday.'

'When is mom coming home?' Nari asked

'I believe your dad will fetch her on Saturday.'

Nari nodded his head 'I think she will be happy to be at home.'

'Where will you go to Site?' Mia asked.

'I am still waiting for comfirmation Mia, but first I want to have a short holiday in Tokyo, so I can see more of your lovely country.'

'You will love it there Site.' Nari said. 'There is so much to see and do. I will make a list of the places you have to go to.'

'Nari, that is nice of you. I will certainly use your recommendations.

How soon can you let me have the list?'

'I will get it ready for this evening Site then I can explain to you what it is all about.'

The children stayed a while longer and then left Gail in the garden. She was reluctant to go inside feeling that she would not have the opportunity to be in the lush garden again and the thought saddened her. She took a deep breath and got up from the comfortable chair and slowly walked through all the flowerbeds. Their exotic fragrances lingered as she passed, and she tried to lock their perfume into her very soul.

That evening after dinner Gail set up her laptop and showed Nari and Mia how to connect to e-mails. Then she went with them to their computers and after practicing a few times, they had all the connections in place. They had a lot of fun as they sent messages to each other and to Gail, and when Whan and Fing wanted to join in, they were shown how to press the buttons on the keypad. Gail knew that the little ones would soon be able to communicate and wondered whether they would remember her after a while. She smiled at the thought knowing how quickly children adapted.

The next day was Wednesday and Gail knew she had to slowly withdraw from the children no matter how it pained her. She asked Mr Ming the driver to take her to the village and she spent time walking around and buying small gifts for the children and for Nahne.

She also bought a soft leather money pouch for Mr Ming and had it gift wrapped which she gave to him when he fetched her.

'Thank you Mr Ming' Gail said 'for allowing me to see your beautiful country. I will always think of you as my guide.'

Mr Ming bowed very low and his eyes did not meet hers but instead rested on her hands. 'I am the honoured one. You have made me a part of your life and I will also never forget that.'

Gail walked to the car and waited for Mr Ming to open the door not looking at his face. They each knew that in their own way they were both honoured.

The next day found Gail being less and less noticeable as she prepared the children for her departure. She wanted it to be without stress and she also needed the time to make her own adjustments.

On the eve of her departure Mr Lai asked her to join him in the lounge after dinner. He sent the children to their rooms where Nahne prepared them for bed.

'I have prepared all your travel arrangements for your stay in Tokyo.'

He handed Gail a thick envelope which she thought of opening but he stopped her before she could.

'Wait until you are in the car tomorrow before opening it.' He looked into Gail's eyes and she quickly dropped her gaze not to be disrespectful. 'Everything is in order and checked by my secretary so you will have no problem. We, my wife and I, wish you much happiness for the future but most of all we want to thank you for being a true grandmother to our children when they needed one.'

Gail was emotional but somehow managed to speak. 'For me it has been a great privilege to be a part of your family. I will keep the children in my thoughts always, and I wish happiness and good health, for your lovely wife.'

Gail stood up and left the room. She walked slowly to her suite and put the envelope into her travelling bag. Mr Lai had asked her to keep it closed until she was in the car and she would honour his request.

She sat for a moment and then went to the children to say goodbye. Gail went to each one, but did not stay long, so as not to upset them.

In her own room she recalled the past few days and lingered on all the different events that had taken place. She saw the faces of the children filled with excitement and the gifts they bought for her that were now safely packed in her luggage. Her own sadness was overshadowed by their smiles and hugs and she had marvelled again at the flexibility of the young. Sa Ami had taken her to town and bought her a selection of new garments and then they had lunch at their favourite restaurant. Gail recalled each word that was spoken as if it was happening right then.

'We will all miss you.' Sa Ami said. 'We have come to rely on you for so many things. I have bought you a gift which I hope you will enjoy.' Sa Ami took out a small box from her handbag and put it on the table.

Gail felt again how her eyes had misted up and how she had wiped a tear away and how her voice had been heavy with emotion when she spoke.

'I have loved being here with you all and this time for me was a highlight in my long life. I was nervous when I first came but you made me welcome. I found a special peace here and will take it with me wherever I go.'

Carefully Gail had opened the little box and when she saw the contents it had taken her breath away. How did Sa Ami know? This was the first thought that entered into her mind, and then she remembered that she had once mentioned to the children that it was one of her dreams. The ring on the bed of velvet glistened with tiny diamonds surrounding a most beautiful emerald stone. Gail had never seen such a large stone of genuine emerald and for a moment she was hesitant to take it out of the small box.

'Try it on.' Sa Ami said. 'It should fit but one must be sure.'

Gail had taken a deep breath and then delicately taken the ring from the box and slipped on her finger. The fit was perfect and she had felt her heart beat faster. She had closed her eyes too afraid to believe what she was looking at. When she had opened her eyes and saw the ring still on her finger, she looked at Sa Ami smiling at her.

'It is beautiful, and I cannot believe that it is mine.' Gail remembered saying.

'I have a friend' Sa Ami had said 'in the jewellery trade and he sourced the stone especially for me. I wish you much happiness in wearing it.'

Now as Gail stood in front of the window in her room she held her hand up and admired the ring once again. She had done this many times in the past few hours and the pleasure in looking at it was always amazing. She knew that it was by far the most beautiful possession she had ever owned and it made her feel fulfilled in a strange way. For her, material things had never been of great value but this ring felt as if it was always meant to be on her finger.

Gail knew she was a loving person and that was precisely why emotion was one of her biggest problems. She longed to see her family on a regular basis and they had never understood how important it was to her.

She also knew that wherever she was in the future, it would never be a permanent place and she had no problem with that. In fact it was better to have short stints rather than long ones. That way one did not become too attached.

Chapter Fourteen

D AYLIGHT WAS FADING AND lights came on like fireflies as Gail sat on a chair looking out of the window in her hotel suite. Earlier she had, had a shower, and dressed putting on one of the new kimonos that Sa Ami had bought for her. Mr Lai had made impeccable arrangements for her holiday in Tokyo, and had arranged for a guide to escort her, to see some of the night sights. Gail was grateful to Mr Lai for making everything so easy as the size of the city, and the masses of people, were daunting.

A short while later Gail got up to finish her dressing, wondering where she would be taken to. Her kimono was charcoal with grey embroidery in lighter and darker shades, with wine red swirls that brightened the dark colours. On her feet she had on charcoal satin shoes with a red band crossing over the front of the shoes. Her whole appearance looked smart and classical when she looked at herself in the mirror. Finally she clipped the black comb in her hair. A woman who did not want to attract any contact always wore a black comb, while coloured or glittering combs, would indicate that an approach would be welcome. Chuckling to herself, Gail marvelled at all the new ways that she had learned.

Everything was so different in each country and yet it made perfect sense to her.

Looking at herself in the long mirror framed in gold, it was nearly impossible to recognise the woman who had first come to Japan. Not only had her looks changed but her whole manner was transformed.

She was expecting the knock on her door and picked up her small clutch bag that perfectly matched her dress, from the lacquered table.

An Asian man of medium build stood before her. In a glance Gail saw that he was smartly dressed in a dark grey suit with a silk white shirt and black patent leather shoes. He bowed to her and she inclined her head as she closed the door behind her. She thought him to be in his early sixties but was not sure and she smiled with relief when he addressed her in English.

'Good evening Madam. I am honoured to be your guide for the evening. My name is Yung.'

'Thank you' Gail said 'my name is Gail and I will be pleased if you would call me that.' She hesitated then spoke again. 'It has been a very long time since anyone called me by my name and I have missed hearing it.'

Yung smiled and bowed again. 'Then I shall call you Gail if you will call me Yung.'

An array of vibrant colours and sounds met them as they exited from the hotel. It felt to Gail as if there were no spaces in the whole of the universe as everything was filled with colour and sound. People and cars were blended into a teeming mass.

A car was waiting for them at the entrance and the driver slowly turned into the traffic. Excitement filled her very being as she tried not to look too amazed. After all, Gail had been to many beautiful cities but somehow the beat of her heart became faster. What and absolutely wonderful feeling she thought. Who would ever have believed that she could be in this place, in the evening, with a handsome stranger by her side. Gail wondered if Mr Lai used the same service when he had visitors from other countries.

The restaurant was in a quieter area and Gail could breathe slower again. The building was low and nestled in a garden with lights leading up the driveway. The fragrance from exotic flower bushes along the path was overwhelming and Gail knew that she would miss the heavy fragrances that she had become used to in Japan. She had in a certain way become more aware of her senses and enjoyed knowing that fact.

The dinner was excellent and took nearly three hours. They chatted about many things and at the end of the evening Gail had learned that Yung was a touring guide as well as an escort for special clients. As Mr Lai was a very important client he undertook all the assignment that were required by him. Yung was also a junior partner in the tourist agency and hoped one day to buy out the aging partner. He also asked Gail many questions of her work and her family and the time they spent together was pleasant.

An escort was also arranged for the next day but Gail was told by Yung that a woman would be going with her in case she wanted to do some shopping. Gail was happy to hear that as she had in mind to get some gifts for her family.

When Gail returned to the hotel room it was like a haven of peace and calm and after a warm fragrant bath got into bed where sleep came instantly.

After breakfast in the big dining room the next morning Gail took a slow walk in the well tended gardens. Everything was so lush and exotic and very different from her own home where the wind was fierce and only low growing plants survived. She saw it was still a while before her guide would be arriving so she went inside to explore the hotel more thoroughly.

Gail was intrigued with the many salons they had on offer and she promised herself to make use of some of them before she left.

At eleven o'clock Gail met her guide for the day in the entrance of the hotel. The woman was quite young and her English was faultless, as she went through the list of places, where they were going to.

They went to one interesting place after another until Gail felt her legs could walk no more, before they stopped for refreshments.

Although they chatted constantly it was not the same as the night before with Yung and Gail was happy to cut the last few places from the list and go back to the hotel to rest.

That evening Gail dined alone in the dining room and afterwards sat in the lounge in a quiet corner sipping her tea. She thought of all the interesting places she had gone to during the afternoon and made a mental note of those that she wanted to visit again. The gifts she bought for her family were special but there were still some to get and she needed to do this on a slower pace.

It was the morning of the third day, and Gail left the hotel on her own. Without any problem she found a cab a block away and he dropped her off in the centre of the city. She took her time to look more intently at the smaller shops where the most alluring items left her speechless. She was careful in what she bought considering that it would have to be sent by parcel mail and she also knew the weight could not be too heavy.

By lunch time she had gifts for everyone on her list and found a small restaurant where she sat at a table partly obscured by a huge plant.

All the items on the menu had English translations in brackets so it was easy to place her order. Looking unobtrusively around her she scrutinised the people at each table analysing them as friends or business groups.

Voices from a nearby table made Gail aware that they spoke a language that she had not heard for a long time. She pricked her ears to listen more intently and smiled to herself thinking how she had missed hearing her own home language. She turned slightly to look through the leaves of the plant to see where the voices were coming from and saw a man who could be in his forties with two teenagers. The boy looked about fourteen or fifteen and the girl around twelve years of age. Now that she placed them it was easy to follow the conversation. So engrossed in listening to them, Gail was surprised when the waiter appeared with her meal and she turned her attention to her plate of food, but put her fork down again, as she heard the girl begin to cry.

'Hoekom papa, hoekom kan ons nie alleen bly nie?'

'Jy weet tog Yvette, dit is onmoontlik. Ek moet eenvoudig gaan dit is belangrik en ek kan julle nie alleen agterlaat nie, ek kan net nie, al wil ek.'

Now Gail's interest was aroused and she tried to unobtrusively look at the family more intently. The young girl seemed very upset and she saw her wipe her eyes with a tissue.

'Wat van die opvoering by die skool? Papa weet hoe hard ek gewerk het om die rol te kry en nou kan ek dit nie doen nie. Dit is nie regverdig nie.'

Up to now the son had not said anything but now he also spoke.

'En wat van my, ek is gekies vir die eerstespan en nou moet ek dit net so los. Wat van Gia kan sy nie by ons bly nie?'

'Ek het reeds vir haar gevra en sy gaan nie hier wees nie. Ek is jammer maar daar is geen ander uitweg nie.'

Gail's reaction not only surprised herself but the man sitting with his children. She had gotten up without realising it and now stood at their table.

'Verskoon my voorbarigheid' she said as the man looked up 'maar ek kon nie help om julle gesprek te hoor nie. Miskien kan ek help?'

To say a feather could knock one out is a true saying because even a speck of dust could have floored the man. He saw an elderly woman dressed in a peacock blue kimono with a black comb in her hair who spoke Afrikaans and who was offering her help. His mouth was hanging open and realising it he closed his mouth. He got up and pulled out the empty chair at their table and indicated with his hand that she should sit down. Gail sat down and introduced herself and told them of Mr Lai for whom she had worked and that she was on holiday in the city.

The man had regained his composure while she spoke and after introducing himself and his children told her that he was divorced and that the children stayed with him. They had a housekeeper but she was away for a few days to visit her sick son, and he had to leave unexpectedly for work, and now the children had to go with as there was nobody to stay with them.

A dish was placed in front of Gail who looked up surprised at the waiter who unfazed by her changing tables, had deftly arranged a place setting for her.

Gail explained that she would be happy to take care of them until the housekeeper returned and saw the children wait in anticipation to hear what their father said.

Retief Cronje and his daughter Betsy and son Gerhard chatted while they ate their food and after the dishes were cleared away agreed to meet Gail at her hotel that evening.

After informing the receptionist that she would be away for a few days but would be back, Gail waited in the lounge. Whatever prompted her to get herself involved she did not know and to be totally honest with herself she was more than a little nervous.

He was alone and Gail saw in his face that he was mildly impressed with her lodgings.

She got up and picked up her small bag but he was quick and took it from her. She carried her handbag and the briefcase with her laptop.

The cab that he came in was waiting outside and the driver opened the door when he saw them. Retief helped Gail into the back seat and then got in beside her.

As they drove he told her more about his family and commitments and she told him a bit about herself. By the time they reached his apartment they were both more relaxed.

The children were waiting for them and had prepared a tray with four cups and a plate of small pastries.

'Kom sit tannie.' Betsy said

'Dankie' Gail sat down 'julle kan my 'Site' noem.'

She saw the bewildered look on Betsy's face and explained that Site meant granny in Lebanese.

The children were happy and Retief asked if he could call her that as well. 'Natuurlik, dit sal my gelukkig maak.'

Gail asked the children a few questions and they soon had a schedule of duties written down and then Betsy showed Gail around. The apartment was spacious and from the lounge and dining area, doors led to four bedrooms, with the master bedroom at the end. Her own bedroom was a comfortable size with a bathroom and small lounge area with a wrap around music centre covering the walls.

The music centre consisted of a large flat screen television with numerous technical attachments that Gail did not know what their functions were.

She saw that her small bag and briefcase were already there and she smiled to herself as she wondered how her next few days would evolve.

The other bedrooms had similar installations as well as very modern computers and even more attachments. It was very clear to her that the latest technology was right here and then she remembered what field of work Retief was in. He had told her in the cab that he was in technology but she thought he was referring to food or chemicals.

Well now she knew that it was not, and she promised herself that she would know the function of each and every item before she left.

Retief told them that he was leaving very early the next morning and would be gone by the time they got up.

Gail was settled in her room with her laptop open on the bed when he knocked and asked if he could come in. He held out an envelope to Gail explaining that it was some cash in case they needed anything or wanted to go out to dinner or movies. His business card was also in the envelope in case she needed to contact him. She saw him look at her laptop with interest and then he smiled at her.

Gail awoke early the next morning and felt strange and somehow disconnected. She dressed in her kimono and went to the kitchen where Betsy was busy preparing breakfast. Gail realised that Betsy had taken on the roll of her mother and for some reason it made Gail feel sad. Gerhard joined them and the three of them ate breakfast together. Betsy had also prepared lunches for them to take to school and Gail wondered how a mother could let her daughter be away from her at such a crucial age.

Gail packed the dishes into the dishwasher and cleared the table while the children went to fetch their school bags.

'Bye Site' they shouted on their way out.

There was of course a housekeeper but she would be away for a few days so Gail tidied the kitchen and the bathrooms and lastly the bedrooms where she only made the beds. When she was finished she fetched her book from her room, and settled herself on the vast balcony overlooking the bustling city. A soft breeze was pleasant on her skin and she sat like that for a while with the unopened book on her lap. The view was multi layered with cars and people moving constantly below her in a frenzied manner. Shops with their multicoloured neon signs vied for attention and the noise coming from the street below sounded like waves crashing on rocks.

Looking over the buildings Gail could see mountains far away in the background.

Her mind became a feather that drifted high above the city towards the mountain tops where it swirled in total freedom carried by the wind. How lucky she thought, to be here at this beautiful time of the year, and knowing that she was in fact living the life that she had always dreamt of.

When the children arrived from school their lunch was ready for them.

They chatted to Gail, as they ate with Gail who prompted them to tell her about their day and they responded in an easy manner. After the children had changed they sat with Gail in the lounge to talk about their plans for the evening.

Betsy was taking the part of the main character in the school play and was delighted when Gail agreed to go with Gerhard to see the play.

Fortunately Gail had at the last moment before leaving her hotel, included her best kimono, with matching sandals and comb that she could wear to the event.

Betsy was excited and nervous at the same time and chatted to her about her role. Gail enjoyed being with the girl as she helped her to get ready.

When Betsy picked up the brush to do her hair Gail took it gently from her hand and began brushing in downward strokes. She saw in the mirror that Betsy closed her eyes and wondered if she was thinking of her mother.

Gail dressed carefully making sure everything was how it should be.

Her kimono was a rich champagne colour with swirls of green and gold and her shoes matched perfectly as did her charcoal comb with a small row of diamantes down one side. On her finger was her beautiful emerald ring. The children were impressed when they saw her and said so, which made Gail feel pleased and confident.

Their cab was waiting for them and deftly drove to the school where the play was being performed. Gerhard sat upfront with the driver with Gail and Betsy in the back. Seeing him like that reminded Gail of Nari and she wondered how they were getting on.

The hall was packed and Gerhard had a seat with his friends towards the back while the seat reserved for Gail was closer to the stage.

When they first arrived Gail had gone with Betsy to the back of the stage where they were preparing for the performance. When Betsy introduced Gail to her teacher as her grandmother she was pleasantly surprised and had felt at that moment as if she was indeed there with her granddaughter. The same feeling was still with her as she watched the performance on the stage. Betsy gave such a convincing portrayal of her character that Gail felt completely drawn into play. How, she wondered, could any mother not be there to witness her child's greatest moment? Gail also knew without any doubt that there was a specific reason why she had to be here, and that the universe had indeed had something to with it, and she felt tears well up in her eyes. This was life, this moment in time, and she was living it for herself and for the young girl on the stage.

When the performance was over Gail went backstage again and hugged Betsy. The teacher came over and congratulated the girl who Gail saw was near to tears. She put her arm around her shoulder and together they walked to the foyer where refreshments had been laid out.

Parents and pupils were milling around with plates of eats in one hand and a glass in the other. Gail was surprised to see such a mix of nationalities together. Betsy saw a friend of hers and called her over to meet Gail. 'Colleen this is my grandmother that I told you about. She came especially to see the play.'

Colleen was an Asian girl with a lovely smile and Gail recognised her as one of the other performers, and she extended her hand to the girl.

'Hi Colleen I thought you were wonderful.'

'Betsy has told me so much about you.' Colleen said 'I am very happy to meet you.'

Gail smiled at the girl 'I am so happy that I could be here to watch such a great performance of both of you.' She was pleased to know that Betsy had a friend at school and promised herself to find out more about the children before she left.

Gerhard joined them and introduced his two friends. Later some of the teachers also came to compliment Betsy who introduced them all to Gail as her grandmother.'

In the cab going home the children chatted while Gail was content to listen.

The next day would be Gerhard's turn. He had not invited them to watch his match and Gail knew it was a boy thing. After all she had raised three sons of her own. He was just happy to be able to be there playing with his team.

Betsy had made a lovely breakfast the next morning, and after eating, Gerhard went to fetch his sports bag. He made a last minute check to make sure that everything was there, and then with a wave of his hand, was gone.

When Gail and Betsy had cleared up and finished dressing they went down to where a cab was waiting to take them to town for some shopping. The arrangement was made in an easy manner as if they both wanted to be in each others' company.

Later that afternoon they sat at a small table in a restaurant that seemed less busy than others, and Betsy was pouring out her heart. Gail was taken aback with this sudden flow of words and listened while sipping her tea. Betsy missed her mother and she knew her father was lonely and she wished they could be together again. Betsy was crying softly and Gail waited a while, then gave her a tissue and took her hand.

'Julle moet geduldig wees. Gee julle ouers net 'n bietjie tyd om hulle gevoelens onder beheer te kry. Daar is baie probleme wat kinders nooit van weet nie.'

'Maar hulle is lief vir mekaar Site.'

They sat a while longer enjoying each others' company before they left.

Arm in arm they walked to where the cab was waiting.

Although Gail had known this family for only two short days she felt as if they somehow belonged together.

They arrived home shortly before Gerhard who joined them in the kitchen with a huge grin on his face. 'Ons het gewen' he said pushing out his chest. Betsy laughed and Gail laughed with them. She listened as brother and sister chatted about the events of the weekend and left the two alone. She went to her room and looked again at all the attachments on her television. She brought the chair from the small desk to sit in front of the television so she could analyse the objects more closely. She saw Gerhard in the doorway and beckoned him to come and help her. Slowly he explained what the function of each item was and how to use it. Afterwards he let Gail operate it on her own while giving her instructions. She was flustered at first but after a while felt more confident.

Later Gail went to the kitchen and prepared supper for the three of them.

She did not say much except for a remark now and then but enjoyed being part of the small group. When everything was cleared up they exchanged e-mail details and promises to stay in contact.

Retief was due back by two o'clock the next day and Gail had arranged for a cab to fetch her an hour later. She wanted to make sure that she had some time with Retief before the children arrived from school. The piece of paper with the e-mail details of his wife was safely in her bag. Gail intended to send a friendly greeting as well as a report of how the play went and how good Betsy performed. She knew Betsy would send an e-mail but doubted that she would tell her mother how good she was.

He arrived with his bag and a wrapped gift for Gail. She had prepared a tray with tea and they sat in the kitchen in a relaxed manner. When they had finished their discussion he handed the gift to her together with an envelope. Gail did not expect anything and said so to him but he insisted saying that she had been more valuable to him than she would ever know. He helped her with her bag to the waiting cab and waved as they drove away.

Chapter Fifteen

WHEN GAIL GOT BACK to her hotel the receptionist gave her three messages written on notes. The dates on the notes were for the three days that she was not there and Gail realised that although she had told the hotel receptionist that she would be away she had not left any contact telephone number.

The messages were from Jake her eldest son and Sarah who had sent two, one after another. She would have to send them an e-mail as soon as she was settled in her room.

She put her bag and her wrapped gift on the bed and began to unpack. This did not take long and then she carefully opened her gift.

What she saw took her completely by surprise. A large silver gift box revealed a beautiful soft blue leather computer case with her initials foiled in silver in the one corner.

Carefully Gail took the case from the box and zipped it open to find a blue colour laptop computer. Her emotions overcame her and she sat down on the bed beside the box. When she opened the top it was a masterpiece of modern science. It was beautiful and she knew she would not be able to work on it without some help. Somehow she knew that it had been personalised especially for her and she stroked the soft leather case again. One more thing she would have to master she said to herself and she smiled in anticipation.

First she knew she had to make contact with her children so that they could rest assured with the knowledge that she was alright. Instead of sending an e-mail message she decided to give them all a call on the telephone. She very seldom did this but today she needed to hear their voices.

'Mom!' Jake answered on the first ring 'Where have you been? We were worried sick that you were ill or something.'

'I am fine Jake. Just went away for a few days. I will send you a detailed message on the e-mail. How are you all? I miss you.'

'We miss you too mom. When are you coming home?'

'I am thinking about it and will let you know.'

'Don't wait too long mom. I have another call waiting so I have to go. I will watch for your e-mail.' And then Jake was gone.

Gail sat for a while to recall the things Jake had said. She heard his voice again and tears welled in her eyes without her even noticing. She missed him intensely at that moment.

Sarah was more breezie when she answered her telephone.

'Oh! Hi mom! Where have you been? Jake called to ask me where you were and I did not know what to tell him.'

Gail chuckled to herself. The same Sarah never lets anything faze her. 'Are you OK Sarah? I have been thinking about you a lot lately. How are the children?'

'Ag, mom you don't want to know.'

'Sarah I will be sending you a detailed e-mail so watch out for it.'

'OK mom, speak to you later.' And Sarah was gone.

Gail shook her head where she sat thinking about Sarah. Her only daughter and yet there had never been that feeling of togetherness that she had so briefly felt for Betsy. She felt sad as the thought crossed her mind that it had not been Sarah who was at fault but she herself. Gail pondered this revelation and promised herself to be more supportive to her daughter. So deep in thought she was that she had completely forgotten to telephone her youngest son Gavin.

Gail decided to take a walk to get orientated again. She felt at a loss of what to do or where she should go to and although she still had a few days left at the hotel she was restless. She freshened herself up in the bathroom and was sorting out her bag when her telephone rang. 'Hello' she said.

'Mom? Is that you?' Gail felt her heart constrict as she realised she had not spoken to her youngest son when she called the other children.

'Gavin! What a lovely surprise. How are you?'

'Gee Mom, you had us worried there. You must never just disappear again. You know it is difficult for us to get to you in an emergency.'

'Well, no need for anything like that I am quite fine. I went away for a few days and forgot to let you all know.'

'When are you coming home mom? We miss you.'

'And I miss you more than you could ever know.'

'So are you going to do something about it then?' Gavin said.

'I will think about it and let you know.'

'And mom, I love you.'

'Oh Gavin, I love you with all my heart. Give my love to all and I hope to see you soon.'

Gail knew she had to sit down for a while before going out and felt overcome with emotion. It was not a good feeling. She longed to be with her children more than anything. With an effort she got up and left the room.

Days of sightseeing and evenings of visiting exotic restaurants and corresponding with a much extended family via e-mail still being done on the trusty old laptop filled the hours. The new laptop in the blue leather case still bamboozled Gail and she knew she would have to get some help before she could utilise it. She was leaving this for later as her days and evenings were filled with vibrant destinations and interesting guides.

There was only one day left of her amazing holiday and she sat on the balcony of her room letting her thoughts run free. Being on holiday she had not placed any advertisements on the internet as she did not want to be pressurised into anything before she was ready. She knew she had to make her mind up as to her next step but she felt uncertain and too relaxed to do anything.

There was the feeling that she should return home for a visit with her family that kept popping up. When the thought first came up she did not take too much notice of it but somehow it was as if her inner body kept sending out similar feelings.

On her bed Gail had arranged the gifts that she thought of sending to her family and checked again to make sure that she had not forgotten anyone. A roll of bubble wrapping with binding tape was on the floor for her to pack the gifts into. All this would then go into the box that stood on the floor for the courier to collect the next morning.

Her imagination conjoured up images of her children's faces when they received their gifts and Gail felt like crying when she saw how excited they were.

Gail lifted the receiver of the telephone and asked the reception to get her travel agent on the line. Travel agents did not have regular office hours and worked in shifts to enable bookings to be made at any time of the day or night.

When the agent called Gail gave the details of her open ticket that Mr Lai had given her and within minutes everything was done.

Excitement coursed fiercely through Gail's body and she laughed out loud to herself. Then she remembered the courier and asked the reception to call them and cancel the collection that was arranged for the next morning. She would be the courier that was going to deliver the gifts to her children.

Once Gail was settled on the plane she opened up her laptop.

Should she let them know that she was coming or should she surprise them? In her heart she knew it would be better if they were prepared and copied all three in on her message. 'On my way. See you all soon. Love you lots Mom.' Then she added the flight details and closed the computer. She took out the book she had brought with to sustain her during her flight but found it difficult to concentrate. Her thoughts were with her children and she could think of nothing else.

It was only after dinner was served that her mind became more relaxed and in an organised sort of way she recalled the people who she had met and the places she had been to. Her life had seemed like one adventure after another and was more like a movie script at times but there were the beautiful gifts that she had received that could prove that she had actually lived that life. Her bank balance also looked very healthy indeed and of the woman who had felt lonely and neglected was not much to be seen.

No she was in fact a very sought after commodity and she was not lacking in experience. Besides that she was also very well travelled and had all the stamps in her passport to prove it.

Chapter Sixteen

WHEN GAIL EMERGED FROM the glass sliding doors with her luggage she saw them and her heart filled with emotion. She was just going to call out to them when she realised they did not recognise her.

Instead she raised her hand and waved and the stunned look on their faces should have been caught on candid camera. Gail had worn a soft grey kimono for the journey with matching sandals and a bright blue comb with crystals down the side. There was no similarity of the woman they had left at the airport so long ago. Instead there was this exotic person who brought with her the fragrance of cherry blossoms.

Then Jake was folding her in his arms and she put her head on his chest smelling his familiar after shave and her legs felt like jelly and she clung to him. His voice was hoarse when he spoke and Sarah wiped a tear from her eyes which made Gail smile knowing how her daughter always kept her emotions in check. Gavin waited for an opening and then kissed her and held her for a moment not saying a word.

When Gavin let her go she saw the grandchildren and could not believe that they had grown so much. Bernard was taller than she remembered and had matured from the sun bleached surfer to a very attractive young man. And then he smiled and she saw again the fun loving child she had known so well. Then Laura her daughter-in-law came forward with their daughter Anne and Gail smiled at them thinking what a beautiful pair they made. Anne had her mothers' good looks in a darker version which was more like he father.

Gail hugged them to her and then saw Cathryn behind them. She beckoned to Cathryn to join them in their hug as Laura moved back.

They all walked to the nearby restaurant where they filled two tables.

Refreshments were ordered and they chatted for a while before the younger ones left. They would all meet later with Gail at her home where they could spend some time with her.

Sarah also left with Jake and Laura and Gail went with Gavin who was taking her home.

In the car there were so many things that Gail wanted to ask Gavin but he was asking all the questions so she left it for later.

As they got nearer to her home Gail became emotional with the beauty surrounding them. How had she ever thought of leaving this beautiful place? She felt as if her heart was going to explode as memories flooded through it.

'Mom! Are you alright?'

Gail had not even heard when her son had asked her a question she was so enthralled with everything.

'I am sorry Gavin you must forgive me but my mind was dancing in the waves.'

Gavin laughed at her and repeated the question.

'Are you going to be here with us for a while or are you planning on leaving us again?'

How should she answer that question Gail wondered to herself? She herself did not know the answer.

'I will be here for some time . . . . I think.'

Gavin shook his head in disbelief not saying anything until they stopped at her home.

She sat for a moment just looking at the overgrown garden thinking that she was probably just in time to save some of the plants.

Inside she saw that Bernard had moved some of her things around and everything looked dull with a layer of dust. Were the curtains always so faded she wondered or was it just that she was seeing things differently? She knew she would have to do something about that very soon after all she had the money in the bank that she had lacked before she left.

Gavin put her luggage in her bedroom and said he had filled the fridge and grocery cupboards so she could make a cup of tea before resting.

'Don't worry with cooking anything mom. We are all bringing a dish of food with tonight. Take your time with unpacking and just relax.'

He hugged her again and left.

Gail took his advice and put the kettle on, for a cup of tea.

She sat in the armchair by the window where the sun filtered through the curtains. She was home and the places she had been to, faded away in a mist, as if it never happened.

She went to the cupboard in the spare bedroom where she had stored her clothing and selected a cotton pants with a light top. She looked strange to herself in the mirror and then saw the comb in her hair. Carefully she removed it and put it into her cupboard. She doubted that she would ever wear it again and that made her feel sad.

Leaving her luggage just as it were she began to dust and wipe the surfaces and then she fetched the vacuum cleaner from the garage hoping that it was still in working order. Relieved to find that it was she went from room to room to vacuum the dusty carpets. Her body felt tired afterwards and she sat down again to look at everything more carefully. It was so long ago that she had actually done physical work that she had forgotten to take things at a slower pace. She would have to remember that she reminded herself.

When Gail felt rested she began to unpack her bags. She looked at the clothing on her bed and realised with a pang that she would miss wearing her kimonos. She left the clothing on her bed with each kimono and matching shoes in neat piles. The gifts were arranged in the lounge with a small card on each to indicate who it was for. Perturbed she wondered if her choice had been correct. The children seemed different and not as she remembered them. With a jolt she knew that they had not changed, no it she, who had changed.

All these thoughts of uncertainty disappeared when she took the blue leather case from her bag. She had placed it among her clothing to protect it. She felt sure that the grandchildren would help her to conquer the unknown.

Chapter Seventeen

THE LOUNGE WAS FILLED with chatter and laughter as the family stood around with eats and wine.

Gail sat on the couch with Anne and Cathryn on either side as her eyes scanned the room where her children were chatting to each other. She knew it was not only her that missed being together but them as well. There seemed so little opportunity to meet and visit and she promised herself that she would try to make sure that they met more often as a family. After all, a supporting family was a happy family and being together allowed them to catch up on family events.

They all loved their gifts and Anne and Cathryn were astounded by the array of kimonos on her bed. It was Gavin who took the blue leather case and patiently showed Gail the basics. He promised to come again the next day to take Gail slowly through the more intricate steps.

When they all left Gail had a warm bath and fell asleep almost instantly with a heart filled with the love of her family. She had missed them more than she realised and knew that they had also longed for her.

When Gavin came the next day Gail had more or less put her home back to how she had left it and was enjoying a cup of tea. Her car that she left locked in the garage with a disconnected battery had to be seen to and Gavin was going to help her. Gail had prepared a light lunch for them and once the car was sorted out Gail fetched her laptop.

Patiently Gavin went through the basics again and then took Gail deeper into the program.

'Mom.' He said. 'Where did you get this? I have not seen anything like it. It's very advanced.'

Gail chuckled 'If I tell you the story you will not believe it.'

Now he was even more curious. 'What do you mean that I won't believe it?'

'I'll tell you the story one day if you promise to tell me what you have been doing with yourself.'

Now it was his turn to laugh. 'Maybe you won't believe me either.'

They left it at that not wanting to bring anyone else into their time together.

'I have to leave now Mom. Take your time to get the hang of the computer and when you take the car out you must be careful. Let a service station check the oil and water before go drive far.'

'That was precisely what I had in mind.' Gail said. 'I want to go down to the beach just to chill there for a while before doing anything else.'

A hug and Gavin was gone.

Gail took her time to gather what she needed and thought she would be nervous to drive her car after not driving for so long. She was happy that Gavin had pulled the car out of the garage and saw that it needed a good wash. Without effort she drove out of the estate to take the road down to the beach. She had such a strong yearning to walk on the beach where the sand could curl over her toes that it was almost unbearable.

She did not walk far and sat on a rock to rest and look at the waves.

The mountain loomed like a sentinel on the horizon and ships waiting to dock looked like paintings on a canvas.

The wind was not strong and caressed her skin while blowing away the tears that fell on her cheeks as memories rushed like a raging storm through her soul.

She sat like that until she had calmed herself and then slowly walked back to the car.

Gail settled into her old life as if it was a well worn jersey comforting and warm. The children and the grandchildren popped in and looked at all her pictures and gifts and even asked questions about her travels which sounded to them a bit farfetched and Sarah even said it sounded as if Gail had a vivid imagination but that it was not a bad thing if one did not believe everything. After that Gail changed the subject if anyone asked her about her travels. And as the days passed she herself even began to doubt the fact that she had actually done all those wonderful things.

It was in the evenings when she could take out her blue laptop and send messages to all her friends in those far off places that she let her guard down knowing that they actually did exist.

When Jake arrived unexpectedly early one evening and found answering her e-mails he insisted that she show him what was being sent to her.

They sat together on the couch with the laptop on the coffee table before them and Gail clicked on a message from Ursula. Jake read it with interest and then he clicked on Sa Ami which he also read. He did not say much about the messages and then he logged off.

'Mom, I know I have not spent enough time with you but I want you to know that I am always thinking of you.'

Gail looked at her son and smiled. 'I know that Jake and I love you all very much.'

He nodded his head and got up from the couch.

'Can I fetch you on Sunday morning for breakfast?'

'Of course you can.' Gail said 'I'll be ready.'

'Ok Mom, I'll see you at nine.'

And he was gone.

Gail pondered over his visit and knew that he tried hard to be with her although he was very busy. She realised that her children did love her, and wanted her to be happy, but did not always have the time to entertain her. What she also knew was that she could not spend her days hoping for someone to pop in for a few minutes. Besides she did not want the children to feel under any obligation with their busy lives.

She felt herself returning to that old woman filled with aches and pains, and nothing much to look forward to, for the next day.

Gail went to movies on a Friday when new films began and to church on Saturday evenings so she could sleep a little later on Sunday mornings and she sometimes took a twenty minute drive to the casino, where she would spend some time on the tables, and have a meal before returning home. She enjoyed being able to do all these things but she felt unfulfilled.

She checked her e-mails every morning and read with interest of the news coming from other parts of the world. Her own news seemed to get less and less after the initial exuberance that she had felt when telling everyone about her life at home.

She was happy to hear from Betsy telling her that her mom was spending more time with them.

Gail also tried to make more time with Sarah and Cathryn but somehow they always had something they were busy with or on their way somewhere. Gavin popped in for short visits but after the second week of Gail being home it was just a quick telephone call to say he would see her later in the week. Gail knew Jake was very busy at work and did not want to disturb him and weekends Gail felt she could not impose in their time together which left her much as before she left, quite alone. There was nothing she lacked to live a comfortable life but she needed personal contact with people to fulfil her.

So after such a weekend with the telephone not ringing and no invitation for coffee or a meal Gail made a decision.

She was not going to rush into anything but at the same time she would prepare herself mentally for another project.

On that Monday evening while watching television Gail took a clean sheet of paper and wrote a few destinations down the left side of the page.

She added to this list as the evening progressed and when she was ready to prepare for bed she left the paper on the coffee table to look at again the next day.

After breakfast the next morning Gail took out her computer and searched on the internet for the first three locations on her list. An hour later she had eliminated two and added one more. On the right side of the page she had written notes with some words underlined.

This same exercise was performed over the next two days and by the Thursday there were four definite locations that she would target. As before she would begin with the first two on her list and wait three days before spreading her net wider. Gail mulled over decision for most of the day and it was already getting dark when she opened up her computer.

Carefully she typed in her credentials and work experience as well as her age and the position she was looking for. She checked and re-checked what she wrote and then went to the toolbar and typed in the locations.

When she moved the icon to send the advert she hesitated and instead put it into draft. She would wait until the next day before making the final decision.

The Friday morning was busy as Gail dusted and vacuumed and wiped cupboards down. At lunch time she put the kettle on for a cup of tea and a toasted cheese and tomato. She was tired and sat for a while just looking out of the window. She knew she was procrastinating but felt she needed more time to consider her options.

When the lights came on in the street of the estate Gail took a deep breath and fetched her laptop.

She first went to her e-mails and was surprised to see a message from Mr Lai. She smiled to herself wondering what he wanted to tell her as he very seldom contacted her.

'Good day Gail. I am sorry to trouble you but humbly ask that you treat this message as very urgent.'

Her heart skipped a beat as she read further.

'My wife is very ill and is back in hospital. If it is at all possible that you can come will you please come soon?

Most humble request from Mr Lai.'

Gail sat back for a moment staring at the screen and then her fingers moved swiftly over the keys.

'Honoured Mr Lai please arrange for travel arrangements as soon as possible.

With respect Gail.'

She clicked on the send button and carried on reading her other messages.

Mr Lai must have been busy at his computer because his message popped up as she connected to send messages to her other correspondents.

'Thank you Gail will send details. Mr Lai.'

She logged off and closed the computer and went to stand at the window looking at the lights around her. A feeling of peace filled her and even the knowledge that knew she had to contact her children without delay could not change what she was feeling.

'Hello Jake.'

'Hi Mom how are you? I am sorry I never got to you over the weekend but things were a bit hectic.'

'That's ok Jake I understand . . . . there is something I have to tell you.'

Gail heard how Jake drew his breath in. 'You can't be serious mom.'

He what she was going to say even before she said it and she gave a short laugh. 'You know me too well Jake.'

'Where is it too this time mom?'

She told him about the e-mail from Mr Lai and explained that she would be leaving very soon. When she was finished with Jake she first called Gavin. The result was much the same. Sarah seemed surprised but not upset and Gail thought again of her daughter and how she detached herself from anyone so easily.

Without thinking she began to take out her clothes from the cupboard in the spare bedroom. When everything was ready she took the combs for hair from the shelf where she had put it. She stroked the edges feeling the smoothness in a familiar way. Fate had taken a hand in arranging her future and she would accept it.

Once she had everything ready she put the kettle on to make a cup of tea.

She sipped it slowly pondering her decision. Was she doing the right thing? She was with her family in her own home in a beautiful part of the world and yet could not be content and was at a moments' notice, ready to leave again. She mulled this thought over in her mind and sat down in the chair at the window looking out to her small garden. The realisation when it came was not earth shattering. It was just there plain as day. Her children all had their own families and lived separate lives. They knew where she would be and could contact her at any time. She was not deserting them in any way. Gail sighed with relief and got up from the chair to connect to her e-mail site.

Fortunately her passport was in order and Mr Lai had managed to get a flight for the next evening. She did not expect it to be so soon but it was better that she got it over with. Her fingers on the keys responded automatically as she typed. 'Mr Lai I will see you soon. With respect, Gail.'

Chapter Eighteen

T HIS TIME SHE WAS not nervous with the anticipation of meeting the family as she knew them very well. In fact she could hardly contain her excitement.

Mr Lai was at the hospital and had sent his driver Mr Ming, to collect her.

He bowed low to her when he opened the door of the car and she bowed to him without saying anything. She felt happy and strangely as if she was at home as the car inched through the traffic. Familiar places flashed by and Gail put her head back and closed her eyes as she wondered how Sa Ami was and thinking how nice it would be to see her again.

Nahne was waiting at the door as the car pulled up. A big grin lit up her face and Gail was amazed at how she had gotten used to expressions which had first struck her as unemotional when in fact they were not.

Her room was exactly as she had left it. Mr Ming put her suitcase on the floor and Nahne who followed him began to unpack it immediately.

Gail sat on the bed watching her until everything was in the cupboard and a kimono with matching sandals were placed on the bed. Gail smiled at the anticipation of wearing a kimono again without feeling out of place.

Tea and small cakes were waiting in the kitchen and the two women sat facing each other. They had the knack of communicating without saying very much and when Gail had finished her tea she told Nahne that she would rest for a while before the children arrived.

Gail was waiting for the children at the door when the bus dropped them and when they saw her they rushed to her where she hugged them. They all wanted her attention but it was Fing who held her hand tight and would not let go. Gail picked her up and she put her arms around Gail's neck. They all went to the kitchen where Nahne had prepared their lunch.

It was a happy group around the kitchen table with Gail on the one end and Nari on the other end. Nahne was serving as they chatted away telling Gail of their day at school. The past few months that Gail was not with them faded away as if it never happened.

Mr Lai bowed to Gail and she bowed her head in acknowledgement and then they sat down in lounge. Nahne brought them a tray with two small cups on and left.

'Thank you very much for coming.' Mr Lai said. 'I was concerned that you had already taken another assignment.'

'No' Gail said 'I was at my home with my family.'

'Then I am even more sorry.' He said.

'No need for that, they are all well and busy with their lives.'

'That is good because I fear that my wife will be in hospital for a long while yet. She is very weak and when I told her that you were coming she was happy because she knows the children love you.'

This was a very long conversation for Mr Lai and Gail knew his emotions ran much deeper than what he had said to her.

They finished their tea in silence and Gail left to see the children in their rooms.

Gail knew instinctively that by telling her what he did, he had actually admitted to himself the seriousness of his wife's illness and she knew that he was saddened by the realisation.

She found then all in Naris' room. She sat on his bed and they were on the floor. Each one had a chance to tell her something about what they did while she was away.

When Gail retired to her room she sat for a while in the chair going over the hours since her arrival. It was clear that Mrs Lai was very ill and could be in hospital for some time and even after that would need time get her strength back. Gail knew that if she was to be of more use to the children growing up she had to learn their language. She would speak to Sa Ami about that and ask her if she could recommend a good teacher.

The fragrant bath relaxed her aching joints and sleep came easily.

When Sa Ami arrived just after breakfast the next morning they were overjoyed to see each other.

'I have come to take you shopping.' Sa Ami said. 'I have missed our time together very much.'

'Oh yes! So have I.' Gail laughed and quickly went to pick up her purse.

They sat at a table in the restaurant they always went to and for Gail it seemed as if the time that she was away did not exist.

'Please tell me more about Mrs Lai.' She asked Sa Ami.

'So sad. She tried very hard but her body was too weak and now she is even worse.'

'I am so sorry to hear that. The children must miss her very much.'

'I think they do and they were very upset when she had to return to the hospital. When she told them you were coming back they felt better.'

'Sa Ami I would like to learn the language so I can communicate better.

Do you know of someone that can help me?'

Sa Ami smiled at Gail and took her hand that was on the table.

'Of course I do. I will arrange for a tutor who will call you.

I think that will be wonderful.'

Relieved that she could leave it for Sa Ami to arrange Gail enjoyed her meal. No doubt it would be more difficult that she could imagine but if she could master even a little of the language she would be happy.

When he children arrived back from school Gail was waiting outside in the garden for them. Fing and Whan ran to her and she hugged them.

Nari and Mia sat with her and began telling her about their day at school.

They sat for a while and then went inside to put their bags down and eat.

Everything was as it used to be and the children had their opportunity to talk about whatever they wanted to.

Gail saw that Nari and Mia first helped Fing and Whan with their schoolwork before doing their own.

Mr Lai, she saw, was home earlier in the evenings so he could spend more time with the children before they went to bed. He participated in their games and listened intently to what they said. Gail enjoyed watching them and saw him look pensively at the little ones and sometimes even put then on his knee when they spoke to him.

He had changed from the austere man to a more approachable one and Gail knew that Mrs Lai had made that possible. He needed to be available especially for the younger ones.

A while later Nahne would bring a tray with tea and cookies and then take Whan and Fing to get ready for bed and Gail would leave with them.

Nari and Mia stayed a short while longer and then left Mr Lai to read his newspaper.

Gail first went to Fing and Whan and tucked them in while telling them short stories. Then she chatted with Mia and Nari before retiring to her room. Here she would check her e-mails and send her messages before relaxing in an aromatic bath with candles giving the only light. This was a treat she indulged in every night before getting into bed.

Chapter Nineteen

SU JUNG CAME EVERY Tuesday and Thursday to tutor her. He was a short thin man of middle age with a moustache that hung below his lips. His hair was long and fell forward as he spoke but this did not seen to worry him.

The lessons were difficult and Gail felt drained afterwards but she knew she had to persevere in case she needed to be there for an extended time.

Slow progress was the only mode and she practiced her sounds every morning after breakfast with Nahne shaking her head or nodding in approval.

When it was parent and teacher evening at school Gail could ask basic questions without hesitation. The teachers knew her as 'Site' and she the grandmother of the Lai children and they accepted her with due respect.

On Saturday mornings Sa Ami fetched them with their shopping lists and when everything was done they had something to eat before returning home. Mr Ming the driver, was also re-installed as their guide to take them on outings and these became more varied as the children had more and more input. Gail enjoyed these excursions immensely especially when Nahne went with them. Twice a month Mr Lai would take the children to see their mother in hospital and brought them home in a subdued manner. After a while the visits became less frequent and then it was only once a month. Gail did not like to question them but it was evident to her that Mrs Lai would not be returning soon.

It was after one such visit that she realised she would have to speak to Mr Lai about her permit of residence which would be expiring in the next three months. These things took time to put in order and one could not leave it too late.

Sa Ami fetched Gail to go to the home affairs office for a renewal of her permit. There must have been a few hundred people when they arrived and Gail's heart sank to her shoes. Clearly this would take more time than she had thought. To her surprise Sa Ami walked past the long row of people to the front where she opened up her bag and took out a card which she showed to the person behind the grille window. The man pointed to a door on the side and Sa Ami gestured to Gail to follow her. Sa Ami knocked on the door and it was opened by an elderly man. There was younger man sitting at a desk tapping on a computer keyboard and he got up and bowed to them showing them with his hand to sit down inthe the two chairs facing the desk. He sat down and carried on typing while they waited. Then the printer on his desk spewed out a document and he handed it to Gail to sign. She first handed it to Sa Ami to verify who read it carefully and then nodded her head. Gail signed and handed the document back to the man. Another copy was printed and checked and signed and then an official stamp was stamped on both copies and one was handed to Gail. The man stood up and bowed and they both did the same and left with the document.

Gail was not surprised with the influence that Sa Ami had but was nevertheless amazed at the speed that their business was concluded.

In the car going home Gail took the document from her bag and looked at it more closely. The date it would be expire was three years in the future and although she knew that her stay could be shorter she still felt a twinge knowing that she may well not see her own family for an extended time.

The feeling made her sad and lasted the whole afternoon until the children arrived back from school. She waited for them in the garden when the bus dropped them and hugged Fing and kissed the top of her head. She knew their mother would miss some of the greatest moments in their lives which would be lost forever.

That evening she stayed a bit longer with each child. If she felt like she did on this day she knew it was nothing compared to what the children would feel if they knew their mother would not be with them for such a long while. Gail knew that she should involve them more on a personal basis and that she should be sharing news about her own family.

Back in her own room she opened her laptop and saw that there were many messages waiting for her. Her own messages to all were more intense than usual as she felt the need to participate more deeply. She would in future not just say 'everything fine' but would give her family more personal news about herself. She told them about the children and the garden and Sa Ami and how she loved them all and would love to hear more news and then reluctantly logged off.

Chapter Twenty

NARI HAD GROWN FROM a gangly boy to a tall youth. His black hair fell over his left eye and he had a look of mischief in his eyes. Gail was amazed at how his eyes changed with emotion. If one did not know any better as she did when she first came, all one would have seen were black pupils when in fact, they were anything but pitch black.

He was bending over her where she sat with his school report in her hand.

It was good except for a remark on behaviour which said 'Aggressive'.

This remark surprised Gail thinking that surely a mistake had been made.

The ease with how she read the report did not enter her mind as it came quite naturally. Mr Jung, her teacher, had been excellent and patient and she now not only spoke the language fluently but read it with ease.

Gail made a telephone call to the teacher and to Mr Ming the driver to take her to see the teacher.

He was waiting for her in the small office next to the office where the principal was and after bowing to each other before sitting down asked her how he could help her.

'I saw your remark on the report you gave Nari and wondered why you felt he was aggressive?'

'On a few occasions' he said 'I saw him loose control of his temper.

In our community such a weakness does not go unnoticed and is not condoned. As you know we are a passive nation or rather that is what we try to engender in the pupils.'

Gail nodded her head slightly and he continued.

'Maybe it is because of a girl.'

Gail felt like smiling but kept a straight face. 'Is there such a girl that he shows interest in?'

'Not openly but I have intercepted some glances between them.'

'And' Gail asked 'can I ask if his school work has deteriorated over this time?'

'No, actually I think it has improved.' The teacher rubbed his chin and sat back in his chair in a pensive manner and Gail waited for him to continue.

'Hormones are strong pulses that the young and inexperienced find difficult to control.'

Gail inclined her head. 'I will speak with him.' Then she got up.

All that needed to be said was concluded. The teacher stood up ad bowed and she did the same.

That evening when all the children were settled Gail sat with Nari on his bed and told him about her visit to his teacher. He was not upset as she knew he would not be.

'Site is he cross with me?'

'Oh no, he is happy with you. He can see that you are becoming a young man. One that will need some guidance with emotions and behaviour, but he thinks you will be just fine. I agreed with him and assured him that he could depend on your good behaviour.'

'Thank you Site. I will not disappoint either of you.'\

Gail stood up and kissed him on his forehead and left. She knew he understood what was expected from him.

In her own room she sat looking out of the window at the darkness outside. Thoughts of her own children darted in and out as she picked up snatches of their progression from child to youth and then adulthood.

She knew of many parents who did not understand their children in this phase of growing up and thought their offspring were rebellious and unruly. To her it was an exciting time of a young life that waited like a butterfly to emerge. In fact that young child was confused and uncertain of the rampant feelings that devoured their bodies.

She was sad that Mrs Lai could not take part in the time of her son changing into manhood. A silent tear rolled down her cheek and she wiped it away in a dismissive way. She realised that it was time to give Nari more responsibility so he could feel challenged and in that way overcome his emotions. She had no doubt that he could manage it and smiled. She would speak to Mr Lai and he would know how to put this in place.

When Gail told Mr Lai about her visit with the teacher she saw him trying to hide a smile. He knew the feeling his son was going through and later she saw him with Nari in his room. This was the beginning of a more personal relationship between father and son as Mr Lai involved his son more and more in their conversations. Gail saw the difference in the way Nari conducted himself and she felt proud of him.

November brought with it many functions at school and Gail attended them all. The teachers knew her as the grandmother of the Lai children and always treated her with the utmost of respect. Mia had taken an interest in acting and was one of the main characters in her school play and Gail spent a lot of time with her to get her lines perfect.

Whan and Fing also participated in their school play but took minor roles which only required them to be dressed up and be there. Life was busy in the Lai household and Nahne helped where she could. Although Christmas was not celebrated in the same manner as what Gail was used to it was still an exciting time. She told the children stories of her Christmases gone by when her own children were small and they loved hearing the stories and had among themselves planned a small celebration to co-inside with their own festivities. No bought gifts were to be given and only handmade ones would be accepted. Gail had bought a selection of handcraft material when she was at the shops with Sa Ami and gave it to the children to make gifts. These gifts were made in secret so that it would be a surprise for the one receiving it and afternoons after school found them busy in their room. Fing was assisted by Gail and the project was carefully hidden each time to be taken out again the next day.

Mr Lai was often away on business and when he knew that it was going to be longer than usual he asked Gail to visit Mrs Lai to give her news of the children. Gail was amazed at how she had gotten used to the language and although she knew it was nowhere near perfect she found it easy to communicate with Mrs Lai who was always happy to see her and asked many questions about the children.

When Gail saw her on a visit she saw Mrs Lai propped up in a chair with pillows supporting her. She looked frail and Gail felt her own heart constrict with seeing the mother of the children she was looking after so weak. She knew the woman was missing her children and on impulse told her that she would in future bring one child with her so they could see also see their mother. She also decided and told Mrs Lai that she would do that the very next day which was a Sunday.

When Gail prepared to leave the woman in the chair she got up and instead of bowing went to Mrs Lai and took both her hands in to her own and gently held them. Mrs Lai looked into her eyes and Gail saw such emotion that her own heart filled with love and she decided that she would bring the children as often as she could so they could share time with their mother.

That evening when Gail opened her laptop a feeling of profound sadness filled her. She sat very still for a while to let the feeling pass her eyes not really focussing on the screen. She knew it was the coming festivities as well as her visit to Mrs Lai that brought the feeling on. How she missed her own children and longed to hear their voices. Without going on line she closed the laptop and went to the window where she sat on the chair staring at the darkness. Time stood still for her and then a soft voice came to her.

'My children are lonely.'

Gail turned her head to see who it was that spoke to her but saw nobody and turned back to the window. Was her imagination playing tricks with her she wondered and then she heard it again.

'Look after the little ones.'

She turned around again and felt a chill. She must have sat for too long at the window and should have known better. She took a warm shawl from her cupboard and draped it over her shoulders and went to check on the children.

She found Nari in bed with his reading light on and a book in his hand.

'Is everything alright Nari?' Gail asked.

'Yes Site.'

'Well don't read too long.'

He smiled at her and she left.

Mia was already asleep so Gail went to Whan who was also asleep with his light still burning so she put it of and bent low and kissed his forehead.

Fing was not in her bed and also not in her bathroom and Gail felt a pulse quickening in her throat as she wondered where Fing could be. Mr Lai was out of town on business and Nahne had already retired. She first looked in the lounge and then the kitchen and then went to the other wing where Mr Lai had his room. Reluctantly she opened the door. This was not an area that she ever went to as she regarded it as Mr and Mrs Lai's sanctuary. At first Gail saw nothing in the dark room and then she turned on the light which gave a soft glow from the recessed lights in the ceiling.

Fing was curled up on the bed in such a small bundle that it looked like a scatter cushion. Gail went to the little girl and saw she was asleep. Tears had dried on her cheeks and her little hand was pressed into her mouth.

Gently Gail picked the sleeping child up and held her close as she carried her back to her room. She was going to put the child in the covers when she changed her mind and took Fing to her own room. She put the sleeping child down on the bed next to her and tucked her in. Tonight she would not be alone. Once more she went to check on the other children and saw that Nari was also asleep and quickly had her bath. She felt the little body asleep but tense and put her arm lightly over the child. A deep sigh from Fing nearly broke Gail's heart. Such a little child and although Gail and Nahne was there it was obvious that the presence of a mother was sadly missed. Gail knew that she would have to see what she could do about that as sleep enveloped her.

After reflecting on the evening past Gail told Nahne what had happened and how she thought they could fill the gap to give the children more attention. Cooking classes were top of the list for the girls and gardening was next for the boys. They would have regular duties and be more involved with the running of the house. Special patches in the garden would be demarcated for growing vegetables which the boys would be responsible for and the girls would have one day a week to practice in the kitchen and then one day that they had to prepare a dish for a meal for the family.

The gardener was called and Gail explained to him what their plans were.

He bowed and asked him to follow her to an area on the outskirts of the garden.

'This will be a good place for vegetables because the sun shines here all day.'

Gail agreed with him and asked him what vegetables he would recommend that they could use in the kitchen on a daily basis. He said he would make a list and let her have it.

Next she sat with Nahne and they selected dishes that were not too intricate to get the girls started. When both lists were completed she called the children together in the lounge after dinner and put the lists and the plans on the table.

Mia was excited but Narti was not keen. He felt he did not have the time or the interest for a garden. Gail let the idea simmer a while and gave her attention to Mia. 'This dish is not difficult to make but is very tasty and with vegetables from our garden you know they will be freshly picked. Herbs are always more fragrant when picked in sunlight. Did you know that Nari?' He looked at Gail and she saw a small flicker of interest.

'And in this way Mia you can train Fing and when your mom comes home you can prepare her a meal from freshly picked vegetables from your very own garden that Nari and Whan had grown.'

Then she looked at Nari. 'You know Nari, Whan may enjoy working in the garden and when you are all grown up you will know that you were able to teach him and work with him and that he will be able to make sure that there are fresh herbs for the dishes that Mia or Fing will make for the family.'

These words seem to be the clincher as Nari took a list and read it more carefully.

Chapter Twenty One

ON THE DAYS THAT Gail took the children to see their mother she took one at a time to the room where their mother was. Fing and Whan each had a half an hour alone with their mom and Mia and lastly Nari. Afterwards she would go in alone to Mrs Lai so she could answer any questions that she may have or any instructions of what she wanted for the children.

This arrangement did wonders for Mrs Lai who appeared more perky and smiled more often and it gave Gail more insight of what Mrs Lai wanted for her children and at the same time it gave Mrs Lai a feeling of not being left out while her children were growing up.

On leaving the hospital one day an idea formed in her mind and that evening after the children had gone to their rooms and she was alone with Mr Lai, she breached the subject. He listened intently and then said he would give the matter some thought.

Mr Lai never spoke about it again until a week before the festivities were about to begin.

When they were all in the lounge after dinner and after Nahne had brought the tray of tea he asked her to stay as well.

'Mrs Lai will be home on Friday. She will stay for a week if she is well enough.'

Fing went to him and hugged him and then the children all spoke excitedly.'

'Is it for good papa?' Asked Mia.

'No, we will make it little by little.' He said.

'We will not let her get tired.' Nari said turning to Whan and Fing.

'I know' Mr Lai said 'you will be good as always and Site will be here to help.'

Gail was happy although she knew her role would take a backseat but she knew this was the right thing to do. As a matter of fact she had thought of taking a few days off to do some exploring on her own and later when she and Mr Lai was alone she told him of her decision. She would be near enough to come back at any time but it would give them the opportunity to be alone, besides Nahne would be there. Mr Lai said that he thought it a good idea but stressed that she was welcome to stay.

On their usual Saturday morning shopping trip with Sa Ami Gail told her of her plans.

'Oh that is a good idea' Sa Ami said 'but I have a better plan. I am going away and would like it very much if you would come with me.'

Gail looked into Sa Ami's eyes and knew she would like that very much and said so. Sa Ami was happy with her acceptance and told her about the places they would visit and with each word Gail became more excited. Finally, she thought, she would see the places she dreamt of.

Mr Ming, the driver, fetched Gail on the morning when Mrs Lai would be coming home. Her suitcase was already at the door when he arrived and her excitement made her giddy. She had earlier taken a tablet for travelling as she did not want to spoil her vacation with Sa Ami.

Mr Ming greeted her with a bow and a smile and picked up her bag. She marvelled again at how their relationship had grown over time. They respected each other and had become friends. He was taking her to Sa Ami and then to the station where they would take a train.

Gail had not been to the home of Sa Ami before which was quite a distance away and Mr Ming pointed out places of interest as they drove.

All this was done in Japanese and Gail had no problem in understanding or conversing with him. Another marvel she thought to herself. Here she was in a luxurious car with her driver and she dressed up in a classy kimono and a comb in her hair with tiny precious stones along one edge and sandals to match her outfit and a beautiful emerald ring on her finger but most amazingly was that she was speaking Japanese to the driver. Yes! She thought with a smile, she is a granny and hails from South Africa and she knew now that were no limits other than those one created for oneself.

The stopped in front of a hotel a few streets away from the main town what seemed as a classy neighbourhood. Somehow Gail had thought that Sa Ami lived in a big house but she saw now that it was not. Sa Ami was waiting with her bags in the foyer and Mr Ming put them into the boot of the car. She greeted Gail with a hug and they chatted about their first stop that would be about an hour away. In between Sa Ami would ask a question about Mrs Lai or the children but would then revert again to their holiday.

The hour went pleasantly and Gail saw the vegetation along the road becoming more and lush. She realised that they must be in a different climate zone, and asked Sa Ami about it.

'We are approaching the foot of the mountain where more rain falls so the vegetation is more dense.' She said.

The road became narrower and flowers hanging from bushes were practically on the verge their scent very prominent as they passed.

As they took a turn Gail saw wooden buildings surrounded by the most exotic flowers she had ever seen. They hung in bunches of gold and red and in between them were purple and yellow smaller flowers covering every space. It was so overpowering that Gail felt her heart pumping faster. How was it possible that anything could be so beautiful she thought? And then she heard the wind chimes as the wind softly blew through the leaves. The sound of small bells ringing in unison in waves of music as if it were an orchestra led by a conductor came from everywhere. She felt tears well up in her eyes and her heart expand as the emotion became almost too much to bear.

Mr Ming helped them from the car and Sa Ami took Gail's hand as they walked towards the entrance. No words were spoken as each felt the others' fullness of heart.

Their adjoining rooms looked out over the gardens and a light sliding door of rice paper opened out to a wooden deck that ran the whole length of the building.

Gail went outside and sat on a reed lounging chair with orange cushions.

She breathed deeply of the fragrance of the flowers surrounding her and felt her body relax as if it was in a cloud. She always felt that there should be more to life as she knew it and now she was tasting a little bit of it and it felt good, so very good. She closed her eyes and listened to the chimes that filled the air with their sharp tickling and fell asleep.

When she opened her eyes again it was to see a small table had been placed next to her with a tray with small cups placed on the leaves of the exotic flowers from the garden. The leaves carried with it a scent of an intoxicating smell. Also on the tray was a small covered dish with small biscuits with nuts sticking out from it. Sa Ami came out from her room and sat next to Gail.

'You slept a bit. That is good. Do you feel rested?'

'Yes thank you Sa Ami. Did I sleep for long?'

'About an hour I should say.'

Sa Ami poured their tea from the pot and ate all the biscuits they were so delicious. Everything felt calm and serene and Gail loved how it made her feel.

They sat like that for a while and then took a walk through the gardens where paths crossed going into different directions. The garden at the Lai house was beautiful and well kept but was completely different from the garden they were in now. Everything seemed more green and the leaves of plants looked bigger. Gail mentioned this to Sa Ami who laughed.

'This is a tropical area where pineapples and bananas grow so it is more exotic.'

'Do you come here often Sa Ami?' Gail asked.

Sa Ami did not answer right away and walked faster. Gail was taken aback by her behaviour and wondered what was wrong. She had asked a perfectly ordinary question/

There was a rugged bench under a tree and Sa Ami went to sit down and beckoned to Gail to sit next to her.

'This is only the second time that I am here. The first time was with my husband when we were newly married.' She kept quiet and Gail was just going to say something when Sa Ami spoke again.

'I did not think that I would ever want to come back here but a while ago I had such a yearning to be here that I decided to come as a tribute to our time together.'

Gail wanted to ask Sa Ami more about her husband but was afraid to so said nothing which was just as well because after a short break Sa Ami started speaking again.

'We were only married for four years and had no children. We wanted to travel and had planned to start our family the next year. This was the place that we had come to shortly after our marriage and we had promised ourselves that we would return on our fifth anniversary. Plans were already in place and all the bookings made when the accident happened.' Sa Ami stopped again and Gail waited. 'He was on his way home from work and had stopped to buy me a gift from the jeweller when a robbery took place and he was shot by a stray bullet. The gift was in his pocket and the authorities gave it to me with his belongings.' Sa Ami held out her hand palm down to show Gail the ring she was wearing. It was a dark red ruby stone with small diamonds around it. Gail could not remember that she had seen the ring before and said so.

'I have not worn this ring until now because it reminded me of the pain that I felt in losing him. Today I knew that I should wear it to remind me of the love felt for me. You will see me wear it more often now.'

'It is a beautiful ring Sa Ami and you should let others see how he loved you.'

Sa Ami wiped a tear from her eye and sat still for a short while and then got up.

'Come we have things to do and places I want to show you.'

Chapter Twenty Two

A NIGHT OF ENTERTAINMENT WAS planned for the guests and Gail and Sa Ami were looking forward to it. They had spent the day going for walks and Sa Ami had showed Gail some of the places that she and her husband had visited. For Sa Ami it was like closing a book and Gail felt privileged that she was sharing it with her. Their friendship had reached a more personal level and they were comfortable in each others' company.

They stood on the deck at their rooms and looked at the fantasy landscape before them. Coloured lanterns were lit in clusters of peacock blue, deep purple, bright yellow and emerald and spread deep into the gardens. The scene was so surreal that Gail felt like pinching herself to make sure that she had not died and gone to heaven. There were no words to express the beauty and they just stood and looked for a while.

'Come Gail lets go and join in the fun.' Sa Ami hooked her arm into Gail's arm and together they walked down the stairs.

Sa Ami looked amazing in her peacock blue kimono with matching sandals and colourful comb in her hair. On her finger was a deep ruby red ring that glittered as she moved her hand. Gail had on a more subdued bronze kimono with matching sandals and her comb in her hair was bronze with emerald stones along the side which matched her emerald ring on her finger. They were laughing as they arrived at the long table set in the garden for the guests to have dinner. In the centre of the table was a conveyor belt with small dishes of delicacies on that kept changing as it moved along bringing more and more dishes. The mood was light hearted and grew louder as the small bowls in front of them were continually filled with a clear liquir that was sipped as they ate.

It was a night filled with magic and when they returned to their rooms Gail sat for a while in the comfortable chair to recall the day that was at an end. She felt completely relaxed and content and knew that if she never travelled again she would be satisfied that she had been to this place.

Early morning found the two of them in the salon spread out on their stomachs with warm black stones arranged on their naked skin that glistened with a soft sheen of fragrant oil with soft music coming from within the walls. This was the last phase in their morning treatment session before breakfast. The night before Gail had thought that her body had reached the ultimate state of joy but she was wrong. It was nothing compared to what she felt after the treatment which left her feeling unbelievable light. She thought she felt like a feather and then she knew that it was not a feather but a snowflake/ Yes! That was it. She was a snowflake.

A motorized cart was waiting for them when they emerged from the entrance after breakfast. Rows of compact benches allowed for three people to sit on each and there were already passengers sitting on some.

The women were given a small parasol from an attendant waiting at the cart to protect them from the sun as the top of the cart had been rolled back. When everyone was seated they drove slowly to view the many beautiful places. Gardens with an abundance of flowers and small fountains sprouting from crevices in the rocks and sheer cliffs looming on the sides were a spectacular scene. Gail closed her eyes when the cliffs became too steep wishing instead to be back at the hotel. Near the crest of the mountain the cart came to a stop and everyone climbed out. An area was cleared with benches where one could sit and look at the valley below. The beauty was breathtaking as the attendant pointed out interesting rock formations and plants.

As lovely as it was Gail was relieved when they finally got back into the cart to take them back as height had always frightened her.

The next morning they left for the next part of their journey. A driver took them to a remote village at the other side of the mountain. The vehicle was quite old but sturdy and the drive was pleasant. They arrived at the monastery where they were going to stay for the night in the late afternoon. The road rose up and they could see the walls of the village below them. It looked almost medieval and they could see small figures working in the fields.

The beauty was breathtaking. Intricate patterns were carved out of wood panelling and paintings of vivid colours were all around them. Colours from the high stained glass windows changed constantly as the sunlight shone through them dazzling their eyes. They stood on floors of marble encrusted with gemstones waiting for the attendant to show them to their quarters.

They followed him up steep steps to a veranda entirely created from bamboo. Floor, walls and roof were bound together so close that it appeared as a solid structure. The sleeping area was divided by thin blinds made from rice paper painted with figures of dragons, flowers and mountains capped with snow. Grass mats were on the floor for sleeping and Gail knew she would not do much of that. There were no tables or chairs and their bags were not there. The attendant gave them robes to wear and sandals made from cork and waited while they removed their clothing folding it neatly over his arm. He led them to a large room where high pallets stood in a semi circle. Some of the pallets were already occupied with bodies covered with white towels. Gail and Sa Ami were shown to adjoining pallets and their robes were expertly taken from them while at the same time covering them with a big white towel.

Gail looked at Sa Ami and they burst into laughter making some of the bodies turn their heads to look at them. A little stool was placed at their pallet to help them climb up.

A basin of fragrant water was brought by another attendant who held it while the masseuse sponged their bodies down. Gail was tense at first until the massaging began but this changed almost immediately as firm fingers began at her toes and moved to her calves relieving the tension of the journey. The sound of monks singing in the background made Gail close her eyes to listen more intently and fell asleep. How long she slept for she did not know but when she awoke found that she had been turned over without even realising it. Her body felt light and airy when she was helped from the pallet and she saw Sa Ami was already gone.

With a smile on her face she followed an attendant to where S Ami was waiting with an even bigger smile. Yes! Gail thought. Life is good.

Dinner was an experience that very few people get to experience. In the great hall torches on the wall gave off an eerie light and Gail wondered if they were not afraid of a fire starting.

At least two hundred monks, looking exactly alike, were seated at the long wooden tables. Gail felt a smile creeping over her face as she realised that she looked the same and so did Sa Ami. Their robes were all the same and a rope was knotted at their waist and cork sandals were on their feet. Perhaps the monks were visitors as they were who had come for a cleansing of body and soul and Gail turned to Sa Ami to ask her.

Her voice was almost a whisper and Sa Ami looked surprised.

'Yes these are people on retreat from the outside world hoping for a total re-birth.'

'Is that what you are wishing for Sa Ami?'

'My dearest wish is to emerge from this place as a new person so that I can look forward to a new future. What about you Gail?'

Gail did not answer right away and saw Sa Ami was waiting for an answer. In truth no thoughts of any person or place had entered her mind from the first stop they made. Everything that was, was no longer important and it was only the present that mattered.

'My wish is as yours.' Gail finally answered and she knew it was the truth even though she had not known it before that moment.

A low chanting filled the vast room and they both joined in. A strong pleasant smell of cinnamon and almonds filled the room and lingered on their bodies.

Dishes of cooked, flaked fish were in the centre of the tables with small bowls of oil mixed with garlic were next to each setting with thin strips of bread on the other side. The meal was sparse but satisfying and filled with flavour and they ate with relish.

Each day that followed was a new and unique experience and left Gail with an inner peace which settled layer by layer until it reached her very soul. She was no longer the person she used to be and now consisted of light and air and her body pulsed with a warm current coursing through her very being. Her name was no longer Gail but Sun Goddess and her powers were so great that she could do anything she wanted to. Her feet did not touch the ground but floated on air and a smile of contentment was fixed on her face and she knew she was where she had to be and was who she had to be.

Gail was wrong. The best was still to come as the last leg of their journey was about to begin.

They arrived at their hotel mid morning the next day. It was situated on the outskirts of a village tucked away in a valley. Expansive grounds were manicured to perfection and an array of flowers spread like colourful carpets that seemed to go on forever.

Their rooms overlooked the gardens and glass sliding doors opened up on to a private balcony where two lounging chairs and a small table afforded one privacy while enjoying the beauty below.

The table they were shown to in the conservatory where lunch was served was near a window overlooking the gardens. It was in a tranquil setting with large bowls of flowers hanging from the ceilings and on a raised area near to them two women sat on chairs playing flutes. The music was haunting yet made one feel light and exciting. The lunch was superb and afterwards they went to the bathing area which formed the main attraction for visitors.

When entering through the great wood carved doors a whole new experience waited to be enjoyed. The aroma of fragrant lilies was almost overpowering Waterfalls trickled from suspended platforms into the massive communal baths. Attendants in long silk robes were massaging people on pallets and Gail saw that there women and men with towels covering them. Music came from a group of four musicians on a small platform in the centre. Two women were playing the violin and the men played an instrument that was similar to a guitar, but much smaller. Everything about the hotel was surrounded by music.

A slim woman dressed in a pale blue silk robe was doing a sensual dance of intense harmony in front of the musicians.

Sa Ami led the way to bamboo cubicles on the far side where an attendant handed them a robe and a bathing costume and cap.

They dressed in the costume and Sa Ami took Gail by her arm and together they waded into the bath of enormous proportions. There were other people in the water as well and Gail saw that the water was not too deep as their chests were all above the water. She felt relieved as she did not want to show Sa Ami that she was not only afraid of heights but deep water as well. The water was warm and pleasant and within minutes they were totally relaxed.

They laughed and spoke to some of the people in the water and hardly realised the hours that went by.

'Come it is time to go.' Sa Ami said. 'We have a very special evening ahead of us and we must rest.'

'What are we going to do?' Gail asked.

Sa Ami only laughed and Gail had to leave it at that. No doubt she had a surprise waiting for her.

Gail felt lethargic from the aromatic bath and lay down on her bed to rest for a while and fell asleep. A loud knocking on her door woke her up and when she opened it Sa Ami pushed the door wider and entered with a flat box in her arms. She put the box on the bed and turned to Gail.

'Tonight we must look spectacular so it is best that you begin to get ready. I am here to help you.'

Gail laughed at her friend. 'What do you mean by spectacular Sa Ami?'

With a flourish Sa Ami opened the box and Gail saw that it contained a kimono in a soft peach colour and sandals to match. When Sa Ami took the garment from the box Gail saw that it had gemstones of emerald and tourmaline along the neck and along the bottom edge.

'Oh, Sa Ami, it is beautiful.'

'And' Sa Ami said 'here are the sandals to match and a very special comb.'

Sa Ami waited for Gail in the foyer and Gail smiled at her friend who looked stunning. Sa Ami was like a glittering tower of sparkling gems.

Her face was dramatically made up and the kimono of almost translucent torquise with silver motifs along the edge and her sandals matched beautifully. In her hair was a high comb with silver stars and crystals that glittered as her head moved.

The whole garden had been transformed into a fantasy of lanterns of deep orange to soft yellow shades. Cushions of silk in gold and silver and torquise and ruby red were grouped together with canopies draped with soft muslin tied together at the corners with clasps encrusted with gemstones. In each canopy hung a lantern which gave off light in shades of emerald and ruby.

Women attendants were dressed in silk wraps with open midriffs and gemstone headdresses and gem encrusted slippers while the men were dressed in black tunics and wide trousers with gemstones along the edges of the tunics. Some carried small trays of bite size eats which they offered to the guests while others had trays with the small china cups with saki.

Sa Ami gently steered Gail towards a canopy where two men were sitting on cushions. The men got up as they approached and Gail realised that they were waiting for them. The older of the two was completely bald and taller and Gail judged him to be about sixty-five or seventy and wore a black trouser and tunic with an embroidered dragon rising up from the hem. The sleeves of the tunic were wide and richly embroidered. His shoes were black and the toes were embroidered with gold thread.

The younger man was strikingly handsome and although a bit shorter cut an imposing figure.

They all bowed to each other and then Sa Ami introduced them to Gail.

Turning to the bald man Sa Ami said 'Gail this is Mr Neo Gaan.'

Gail inclined her head and did not look into his eyes. Then Sa Ami turned to the other man and Gail thought she heard a more personal touch in her voice. 'This is my good friend Pavi Fhan' and turning to Gail she said 'and this is my dear friend Gail.' They all bowed again and sat down on the pillows.

Sa Ami had not prepared Gail for company and Gail looked at her in a questioning way but Sa Ami did not notice it as she was talking to Pavi.

Attendants brought trays of eats and drinks and Gail smiled and felt herself relaxing.

His voice sounded rough when Neo addressed Gail and for a moment she did not understand what he said. She lifted her eyes to his face and saw he was smiling at her. 'I am sorry. May I call you Gail?'

This time she understood clearly what he said and she realised that he spoke with an accent that was not from that region.

'Of course if I may call you Pavi?'

Clearly surprised that Gail answered him in Japanese she saw his eyes crinkle on the sides and then he laughed out loud.

'Please tell me who is dressed in this lovely kimono because you look European and yet you speak Japanese. Where do you come from?'

The ice was broken and they chatted freely telling each other about themselves. Sa Ami and Pavi had joined in the conversation and Gail understood that Neo was the uncle of Pavi. It was also clear that Sa Ami and Pavi had feelings for each other as they spoke to each other with tenderness in their voices. There was much about Sa Ami that Gail did not know about and she was taken by surprise on many occasions.

Music filled the air and laughter could be heard from other canopies where people sat together in groups. A jovial atmosphere that was no doubt enhanced by the saki was all around them. As the evening went on, they enjoyed themselves more and more and when Neo asked Gail for a dance she immediately held out her hand. Other couples were already dancing and Gail easily slipped into his arms. It felt good to be held by a man again she thought as their steps flowed in harmony. When she rested her head on his chest for a moment he held her closer.

The night was filled with magic and it was only when the dawn arrived in soft pink shades that the men left after bowing deeply to the women.

Arm in arm the giggling women walked back to the hotel to sleep.

Although the hour was late or rather early Gail did not feel like sleeping.

She sat at the window watching the dawn fade away as she replayed the evening in her mind. She knew that if Sa Ami had warned her she may have re-acted differently and smiled again. She closed the blinds and went and had a warm relaxing bath and fell asleep.

Chapter Twenty Three

THE CHILDREN WERE WAITING at the door when Gail arrived back from her holiday and were excited to tell her about their mom and also to hear about her trip.

Mia and Fing went with her to her room to help her unpack and then they all went to the lounge where Nahne had a prepared a tray with delicious snacks.

'Our mom was much stronger this time Site' Nari said 'she will visit us again when she is rested.'

'Oh! Nari I am so happy. Did she look well?'

Mia chipped in 'She had to rest a lot but we were good and helped her.'

Gail knew that then that Mrs Lai was not ready to come home yet and she hugged Fing who was sitting on her lap.

'You must be patient. She will come when she is ready and we will visit her as often as we can.'

Mr Lai was away on business and when everyone was settled in bed Gail took out her laptop. She had not taken it with her and a whole string of messages flashed on the screen. She went through each one before answering any knowing that some would require the same answer as Sarah would have kept sending the same not having had a reply.

'Where are you mom?' First one of six similar messages. Then Gavin with more friendly messages. 'Tried to get hold of you mom are you ok?'

It was the message from Jake that made her heart beat faster.

'Have to go on a business trip and will be coming to see you. Have found accommodation in a guest house in the village for the week end and will see you soon. Can you arrange for transport from the airport? See you soon. Jake.'

Gail looked at the date and realised he would be there in two days. She was excited as her fingers tapped the keys.

'What a pleasant surprise. I can't wait to see you and will be at the airport with our driver. Love mom.'

The rest of the mail was quickly dealt with and then she sent one to Sa Ami telling her of the intended visit of her son Jake and requesting the service of the driver for the days that he would be there.

Sleep evaded her even though she had relaxed in a fragrant bath. Her feelings were already reaching out to her son who she would see very soon.

She told Nahne of the impending visit of her son and she came to Gail and hugged her.

'Then I will also meet him?'

'Of course you all will.'

'I will make a special dinner for him.' Nahne said.

'He will love that and I know that you will like him. He is a very special son.'

Nahne nodded and Gail saw a tear being wiped away from her eye and she felt again the love that had grown between them.

That evening when Gail told r Lai that Jake was coming to visit her and she him smile which was very rare. For the first time he asked questions about her family and Gail felt she could freely tell him something about her life. The children were excited and later in their room when she went to say good night they asked more questions.

Early on the Friday morning when the shadows of the night were still hovering in corners Mr Ming arrived to take her to the airport.

She was dressed in a light blue kimono with matching sandals and a comb with tiny blue beads along the edge. There was a glow to her skin that made her look much younger than her years. She kept her excitement in check for fear of it getting out of hand lest she be disappointed.

Mr Ming waited outside in a special area reserved for arriving passengers to be collected and she went inside to wait for her son. She sat on a nearby row of chairs until she saw the passengers walking through the sliding doors and then got up and moved closer so Jake could see her.

Her heart skipped a beat when she saw him and she saw him look at the people clustered around but his gaze did not find her. He stood uncertain while she watched and then she raised her hand and waved.

She saw the look of surprise and then he was there and hugged her.

'I did not recognise you mom.' He stood back to take a closer look. 'How is it possible that you have grown younger since I saw you?'

Mr Ming greeted Jake with a bow and a smile as he opened the door of the car. The journey seemed different to Gail as she pointed out interesting areas. She had grown used to the countryside and hardly took notice of the places anymore.

In the lounge where they sat after a delicious dinner prepared by Nahne, Mr Lai was chatting to Jake in a relaxed manner. The children were all there listening to the conversation which was in English and Nahne flitted in and out with trays of refreshment. Gail was warmed by the friendly way they all welcomed Jake and she could see that Jake was impressed \as well. For the very first time she actually heard Mr Lai laugh out loud and she saw the children laughing as Nari chipped in occasionally.

Gail left with the younger children to get ready for bed while Nari stayed behind. They heard the laughter from the lounge as they walked down the passage and Gail smiled with her heart filled with the love for her son.

'Site, why can't we stay a bit longer with Jake?' Mia asked.

'You will spend some time with him but now he and your dad are chatting and we want to give them time together. You know your dad is a very busy man and they may not have this opportunity again.'

'When will we see him Site?' Whan said.

'I will speak to him and see when we can all be together.'

When they were all settled in bed Gail went back to the lounge but did not find the men there. She went to the kitchen to thank Nahne but foud her gone as well and then heard voices coming from the study. Gail had never been in there and went back to the lounge to wait for them. She waited nearly an hour before they joined her.

'Mom, Mr Lai was so helpful in explaining to me how to approach the meeting with my clients in a few days time.'

Gail looked at Mr Lai to thank him but he smiled and waved a hand to brush away recognition. 'Only a small piece of advice that can possibly smooth the way with your negotiations.'

'Nevertheless' Jake said 'I feel more confident.'

When he left, Gail walked out with him. He hugged her to him and smelled again the scent that he used and took a deep; breath to keep it with her.

'I will be away for the next two weeks mom but will come back this way to see you again before I go back. I really enjoyed meeting Mr Lai and the children and the meal was great. Will you please tell the housekeeper that I said so?'

'Nahne will be very pleased. Take care Jake, remember I am always with you. even if I am far away.'

Jake looked at Gail and his voice was serious when he spoke again.

'You are amazing mom, I always knew you were special, but quite frankly I am blown away by what you are doing here.'

At the car he waved again and Gail felt her heart fill with pride. She was so blessed and she knew she was loved by her children. Then again she would not have missed her present way of life for anything in the world.

In the car that was nearing its destination Jake though again of his mom. He found it difficult to see her as his mother when she was dressed in eastern clothing and spoke a foreign language that he could not understand. He remembered her as a down to earth mother who helped her children with their homework and cooked them delicious meals.

Slowly the realisation dawned on him that she must have been lonely although she never said so to them. Their own lives had become so engrossed with their own family that they had forgotten about their own mother. Jake tried to think back when he had last invited her for a dinner or even a cup of tea and he could remember such a time. He felt sad that his mom had to go to another family to find the company that she craved.

Gail did not see him arrive as she was busy in the kitchen with Nahne as they chatted away. He stood in the doorway watching them amazed at the ease with which him mother had mastered the language. He saw her in a new light that had faded away from when he was a child to becoming a man.

His greeting was cheerful and they looked up with surprise to see him there.

Where Jake sat in the lounge with his mother opposite him with Fing next to her, he felt a twinge of jealousy, as he saw how they all loved his mother. They all treated her with respect and he could see that the housekeeper got on well with her even though he could not understand a word they said. The fact that he was going home in two days time and leaving his mother behind made him feel lonely even though his family was waiting for him. He was filled with emotion and felt his eyes begin to water and looked down to gain his composure.

When Gail looked at her son and saw his sadness and her voice was filled with love for him.

'It has been absolutely fantastic to have you hear with us Jake. I am so glad that you could meet the family who have been so good to me. Mrs Lai will soon be strong enough to come home and then I will go home.'

Jake smiled with relief and Gail knew that what she had said was how it was going to be. She was going home and she would be content to be there.